GW00401786

'Don't sacrifice yourself to this job, Sister Anderson.'

'N-no, Dr Adams,' Penny managed to say, but added softly because it was true, 'It couldn't ever be that. I love it.'

'Do you?' he asked, and it made her glance up. His face was turned to her, his look searching.

'Yes,' she said. 'It's not like—like work.' She thought it sounded silly, but when she looked back at him she thought his lips had curved a little—just a relaxation of their normal line. Before she could think too much, she asked, 'Do you have a family, Dr Adams?'

'No. I have an excellent housekeeper who comes in to cook, and after a great struggle I've mastered the reheat control on the microwave.'

Penny gave a spurt of laughter. It was so comic to think of a man like him struggling with something so simple. She glanced up quickly, hoping it hadn't offended him. But it was all right, she thought, His face even held a look of faint humour, which Penny liked.

Judith Ansell is a doctor who has always had an interest in writing. She has worked in many different and sometimes exciting areas of medicine, and thus has an excellent background for writing Medical Romances.

At present she combines part-time medical practice with writing for Mills & Boon, and caring for her unruly two-year-old. She is married to a surgeon, and can affirm that doctors make excellent and patient husbands.

Previous Title

THE HEART'S HOME

CHAPTER ONE

PENNY was lost.

Down the corridor, through the arch, right, then left and you'll see double doors, the man had said. She had followed his instructions faithfully, she thought, but no doors stood beckoning her into the new world of St Matthew's Hospital children's neurological ward.

She looked at her Mickey Mouse watch. Mickey said it was one minute to eight o'clock, and that it was not a good idea to be late on your first morning in a new job. It was unlikely to impress her new boss, Dr Nicholas Adams, the director of the unit.

Today would be their first meeting. It had struck her as faintly curious that the director of the unit had been absent from the employment interview she had attended, but she supposed he had been too busy to be there. The director of surgery, Dr Lewin, had told her that the unit was always overworked. It was this circumstance which had led to their advertising for a nurse counsellor. The clinical workload, he'd explained, was so great that nursing staff had little time for talking to the patients and their families.

Penny could well appreciate the importance of time for talking in a unit where children were often desperately ill or facing major surgery. And talking to patients and families, advising them, giving them comfort, had always been Penny's major interest. She had jumped at the chance of leaving general nursing and training as a nurse counsellor when it had been offered her.

Those who had recommended Penny for the counselling course had no doubts about her ability to do the work, and in the year since then she had proved them right. This job, however, was going to be a special challenge. For almost all of these children were seriously ill, and many were dying.

Penny brushed her straight dark hair anxiously away from her face. Perhaps she should have worn it tucked up. It never would stay behind her ears. It was too fine and glossy. She cast around among the moving throng of nurses, wardsmaids, doctors and porters for someone to ask for further directions. Rather desperately, she chose someone at random, and asked her way again.

This time, no sooner had she turned a corner than her goal appeared before her. Shyly, she pushed her way in through the double-doors, and stood surveying the ward which would become so familiar to her over the next few months.

Well, here she was. But where did she go now? And who to report to? Penny had almost made up her mind to look for the sister in charge when a voice at her side interrupted her thoughts.

'Where are you going, looking like a little lost sheep, or don't you know?'

Penny looked up, grateful for the chance to tell someone. The voice belonged to a doctor, a tallish blond man who was smiling in a friendly way. His smile made her relax a little, and she realised how tense she had been.

'Heavens!' he said. 'A smile of relief, I call that. Have you been wandering the catacombs for ages?'

Penny laughed shyly. 'Well, yes. You could say that. And having found my way here, I'm not exactly sure what I ought to do now. I'm the new nurse counsellor, you see, and I don't know who I should report to.'

The doctor raised his eyebrow. 'Are you?' he said appreciatively. 'Well, things are looking up around here. Welcome aboard. Dr Larry Stevenson, at your service now and at all times.'

Penny blushed at his enthusiastic examination of her, which took in the details of a slim feminine form and an expressive face, framed by dark hair and made especially lovely by a pair of clear blue eyes. She couldn't help feeling pleased at his friendliness. It took away some of the feeling of having come to the wrong place at the wrong time.

'Perhaps you'd better show yourself to Old Nick,' he said, and Penny supposed he was referring to the unit director. She swallowed. Penny had always been shy and uncomfortable with those high up in the hospital hierarchy. She'd had experience of the men who had reached the top of their professions in the medical world. Busy, exacting and often arrogant, they had always intimidated her. But he was right. She would have to meet him.

She let herself be guided a little way down the hall. Perhaps he would be a kind old man, like her father, she thought to herself hopefully.

But the young doctor's next words seemed to banish that illusion. 'I wouldn't expect too warm a welcome there,' he warned. 'I'll come with you for protection.'

There was no time to ask what he meant, for they had come to a halt outside a door.

'Dr N. Adams', the sign said. Nothing more.

Penny's apprehension increased at the sight of it, and she was glad of the friendly man at her side.

'Ready?' he asked, squaring his shoulders as though to face the enemy, and Penny smiled.

'Thank you, Dr Stevenson,' she said, and he made a deprecating noise.

'Larry,' he told her. 'Save your "Doctor" for this one.' And he knocked on the door.

He was not what she had expected. For a start, he was hardly 'old'. Somewhere in his thirties, Penny guessed, which made his achievements the more remarkable.

He was taller than Larry, and dark, and decidedly good-looking. His face was strong and serious, and his gaze uncomfortably penetrating.

Penny managed to stammer some sort of acknowledgement of his greeting, and found herself feeling glad he hadn't been at her interview. She would never have got the job if she'd had to present herself in front of him.

He was courteous, she found, but it was a very formal kind of courtesy that did nothing to set her at ease.

He had asked her to sit down, and was explaining how the unit ran, the sort of patients it had, and the composition of the staff. About her role, he had up to this point said nothing. Penny wanted to ask what was expected of her, but she found him, despite the punctilious politeness, too daunting.

I have a problem with authority, she thought. It

makes me feel like a schoolgirl. It would have given Penny very little comfort to know that at this moment she resembled nothing so closely as a schoolgirl, as she sat nervously twisting her fingers in front of her, with her long dark hair hanging straightly down her back.

Dr Adams voiced her question for her. 'I expect you're wondering where you fit into this picture, Sister Anderson?'

Penny murmured assent and waited.

He paused for a moment, the suggestion of a frown on his face; and his tone when he spoke assumed an even greater formality.

'Dr Lewin saw the need for a person to minister to the emotional needs of our patients and their families. As he must have told you, this unit is always full.' There was perhaps a note of bitterness in his voice as he continued. 'I consider we have insufficient medical staff—both doctors and nurses—to cope with the load. This is clinical work I speak of. There's too little time for talking, for allaying fears, for—dealing with grief.' He stopped a moment and fixed her eyes with his own. They were clear grey and fathomless.

'Many of our children die, Sister Anderson,' he stated, with no alteration in his tone.

Penny's heart did a queer thing. It thumped. Perhaps it was the way he'd said it. She was grateful that he had turned away.

'It is our job to prevent this. But we can't always do it. Quite a small percentage of brain tumours are operable. Operations leave their own damage. We also have trauma cases. Head injuries which are sometimes fatal, often disabling.' His voice had trailed away, and he stood at the window as though lost in the consideration of his own words.

Penny felt she should speak. 'I can see that there will be a lot for me to do here, then,' she ventured bravely.

'Good,' he replied, turning to look at her. 'I'm glad you see that. You'll have to work things out for yourself. No one here has the time to direct you.' Penny was almost sure of the note of bitterness now. He went on, 'I'm assured by Dr Lewin that you're the sort of person who can work independently. Of course, there are social workers in the hospital to whom you can turn for advice and guidance, but I hope you understand, Sister Anderson, that you're largely on your own.'

Was there a challenge in this last sentence? Or—worse—was he somehow displeased with her.

I do have a problem with authority, Penny thought, and shrugged it off. He didn't even know her.

'I can only suggest,' he finished, 'that you get to know the patients we have at the moment. Ask Miss Fosdyke for their files.'

And then he was dismissing her, politely but unmistakably, with a wish that she might enjoy her work here, and asking Dr Stevenson to stay a moment..

Penny closed the door behind her gratefully, breathed a huge sigh of relief that that was over, and wondered who Miss Fosdyke was. She would have liked to have asked Dr Stevenson, but she didn't feel she ought to hang around outside the boss's door, so she took herself off with the intention of introducing herself to anyone who could be got to stand still long enough for the purpose. Perhaps she would run across Miss Fosdyke in the process.

By lunchtime it seemed to Penny that she had met a bewildering variety of people, most of whom had evinced a willingness to be friendly and helpful if only time would permit. Miss Fosdyke, whom she had finally found, turned out to be a rather formidable lady of middle years who would not surrender any files to Penny until she had assured herself that it was at Dr Adams' express command. She was some sort of secretary, Penny gathered, though she had more the air of self-appointed guardian of the person and interests of the unit director. She occupied one end of the long enquiry desk not far from Dr Adams' office, and stationed herself there, it seemed, for the purpose of repelling intruders.

There were numerous nurses, who were too busy to do much more than throw a greeting over a shoulder as they dashed off. But it was usually accompanied by a smile and something like, 'See you at lunch, if I get any!'

Penny had been too reticent to introduce herself to many of the doctors, but some had said hello to her. They seemed as busy as everyone else. There were a number of sisters, one of them a strikingly pretty blonde called Berensen, and a battalion of wards-maids, nurse-aides, orderlies and surgical dressers. These latter inhabitants of the hospital world seemed to have most time for talk, and Penny learned vari-ously that morning that Rose Dyer—wielding a mop in the bathroom—had a daughter at college, that Sam the surgical dresser had an eye for the ladies, and that

Doreen the nurse-aide had the world's worst case of varicose veins.

This latter was also a mine of information on the rest of the staff. Penny heard that Sister Berensen was stuck on Dr Adams, who saw all the staff as pieces of hospital equipment, though at least he was polite mostly—not like some; that Dr Stevenson had a broken heart—a lovely man like him; and that Nurse Ross had left because she was in the family way.

Same old hospital gossip, thought Penny. You'd think they'd be too busy. But Doreen didn't seem to be. In fact, as they stood in the kitchen out of sight of the rest of the ward, she seemed inclined to talk forever, till Sister Berensen came to put an end to it.

'What on earth are you doing with those lunches, Walters?' she demanded, her expression changing as she saw Penny.

Doreen slung the last tray on to the traymobile and wheeled it past Penny, muttering something faintly audible about 'slave-drivers'.

Penny found herself sympathising more with Sister Berensen than Doreen until the latter, with no sign of friendliness on her lovely face, said simply and coldly, 'I hope you're not going to distract people from their work.'

Penny felt her sympathy ebb away. And before she could answer, Berensen was gone.

'Well!' Penny said to herself as Rose the wardsmaid would have said it. 'Well! 'Ow rude!'

When she entered the cafeteria at one o'clock, Penny could see, despite the dire prognostications of the morning, that a number of the nurses of children's neuro had got through their work and come down to lunch. Presumably the rest would come down later, when this lot had finished. She approached their table with her tray with the intention of joining them, but Dr Stevenson intercepted her.

'Hello again,' he said. 'Come and brighten my weary lunch-hour.'

Penny remembered what Doreen had said, and examined him covertly, observing at last to herself that he didn't look like a man with a broken heart. His good-looking face had a very cheerful air, and there were no lines of worry she could see.

'So what did you think of our unit director?' asked Dr Stevenson, cutting in on her thoughts.

'I thought—he was very polite and helpful,' she replied in a non-committal way.

Larry Stevenson made a face. 'Oh, yes, he can be very charming,' he agreed. 'He's one of those rare animals whose bite is worse than his bark.'

Penny had to laugh a little. 'Oh, dear,' she said ruefully. 'Well, I'll have to stay out of biting-distance.'

'Good idea,' he grinned. 'Mind you, I shouldn't talk about him like this. He's all right if you stay on the right side of him. It's just that I have difficulty working out which side that is. Perhaps you'll be better at it.'

Penny didn't feel a burning desire to find out. 'I don't suppose I'll see much of him, anyway,' she said, and settled down to attack her lunch with an enthusiasm Larry said was obscene in a girl of her size.

Larry was easy company. He made her laugh, and told her about himself, complete with the information that he was suffering from a broken heart.

The fact that he conveyed this to her in a tone of unruffled cheerfulness made her doubt the severity of the fracture, but she forbore to laugh, and just said 'I'm so sorry' in a grave voice. Penny was sure that he was laughing inwardly when he replied 'Thank you' with equal solemnity.

Throughout the afternoon, Penny pored over files. Tomorrow, she decided, was soon enough to make the acquaintance of the young patients of the ward. First she would do this much-needed preparation, arming herself with case histories and other available information on children to whom she would later be able to put faces. She sat in a quiet sunny room with windows looking out on to hospital lawns, curled her legs up comfortably under her, and read.

Dr Adams had been right. Many of the children here were desperately ill, and many would die. She had chosen a difficult job for herself, she reflected; more difficult, perhaps, than she had realised. The recovery rate in her last job, in the trauma department of a children's hospital, had been far greater. Often it was simply a case of a gash to stitch or a broken arm to set and the patient went home happily enough the same day.

Penny thought of her own brothers and sisters, all of them younger than herself. Living in a family of nine children had prepared her well to deal with the minor illnesses and injuries of childhood. And even, she reflected—thinking of little Meg who had died— with major ones.

Penny was sorry that she was sitting staring idly into space and thinking sadly of Meg when Dr Adams came to ask her for a file.

Her heart gave a lurch when she saw him, and she swung her legs down from under her.

But he said, 'Don't move. I just want to glance at one of those files. Jessica Brand.'

Hastily Penny found the file and handed it to him, and he sat down with it, apparently intending to read it here. Penny bent her head to the file she had in her hand, but she knew she was too uneasily aware of the boss's presence to become immersed in it again. She hoped he wouldn't take too long.

But it was fully ten minutes before she felt rather than saw him look up, and she looked up herself to find his eyes on her.

'Have you read this one?' he asked abruptly.

Penny nodded. It was really the one that had started her thinking of Meg. The child was the same age.

He seemed to be considering. Finally he spoke. 'One of the hardest decisions in a field like this one is how to answer the patient's questions about his illness. Sometimes children ask if they're going to die. Sometimes the answer is yes. How would you answer that question, Sister Anderson?'

He looked at her keenly, and Penny found his gaze and his query equally disconcerting. It was not that she didn't have strong views on the subject—simply that she was afraid he wouldn't approve of them.

Despite her discomfiture, it was her habit to be honest. Perhaps it was a trait ingrained in her by her clergyman father.

She took a deep breath, and tried to choose her words carefully. 'I think, perhaps, when a desperately ill child asks that question, he often knows the answer anyway. So many circumstances tell him it is so. His parents' concern, the—behaviour of nurses and doctors, and—perhaps children have a sense of it anyway.

I think it might be better in a lot of cases to tell the truth. It has often seemed to me that children can cope better with it than adults can. And even children sometimes feel the need to prepare themselves for death.'

Red-faced by now, Penny waited for the doctor to reply, expecting argument or reproof, or both. It was, she knew, a rather radical stand.

He looked at her steadily for a moment. 'You may be right, in some cases,' he said shortly. 'But it takes considerable wisdom to know which cases.'

She blushed anew, unable to do more than nod her head in agreement. She knew he was looking at her still, and wished devoutly that he would go away.

Her wish was granted. He unfolded his tall form from the chair, dropped the file by her side and, with a 'Thank you, Sister Anderson', was gone.

Penny breathed a sigh of relief. Of all the senior surgeons she had worked for so far, this was one of the most intimidating. He had a particularly discon-certing gaze, she thought.

And yet she could see what Sister Berensen saw in him. He was very attractive. Tall, broad-shouldered and powerful-looking, he moved with an athletic grace, Penny noticed. And if he were only to smile, she thought, his face could be devastating.

She wondered if she would ever see his smile. Somehow he didn't look as though he did it often.

That evening when she left the hospital, Penny was glad to go. The day had been full of new faces and facts, and she felt she could take no more in. She rode home on the bus through the darkening streets, and was happy at last to see the light on in the little

Victorian house she shared with Carrie, her friend from her first job. It meant that Carrie was home. And there was so much to tell her.

'Carrie!' she called up the narrow stairs, and was rewarded by the appearance of a head framed by wild curls over the top of the banister. 'I think I'm going to like it,' she declared. 'It's going to be busy, and hard, and sad. But I think I'll like it.'

'Good,' said Carrie, smiling. 'I never had any doubts, Pen. The job was made for you. Or—maybe you were made for the job,' she added reflectively, as she came down the stairs.

For a moment Carrie looked at the sweet, open face of her friend. It was a face which revealed the person, she thought—warm, loving, loyal. It was a face a child could trust.

Penny had always been a genius with children. Carrie had seen it when they had worked together. She had a way of speaking to them that made them feel safe and understood, and a patience and gentleness that Carrie found beyond her own powers. Perhaps she retained enough of the child herself to know better than others how they felt. If Carrie had any reservations about Penny's new job, they stemmed only from the fear that she would break her heart over the children.

But she was strong, too, Carrie thought. The mouth that was so often curved in a friendly smile could take on a look of firmness and decision. It was not a weak face. It was engagingly expressive; and sometimes it expressed a force and passion that surprised those people who had summed her up as timid and unassertive.

She'll cope, Carrie decided. Whatever happened, Penny would face it squarely in the end, and deal with it. Neither of them knew at that moment just how much there was going to be to face.

CHAPTER TWO

By THE end of Penny's second morning, she was even more certain that she was going to like this job. This morning's work consisted of doing the rounds of the ward, and meeting the young people who had been only names and medical data to her the night before.

It was both a rewarding and saddening experience. The children were pleased to meet her, to have someone to talk to, and from even the sickest child she was able to coax a smile. But the words recorded in their files kept invading her thoughts, and even their cheerful faces could not erase them.

But it was bound to be so at first, she thought. In time she would get used to the thought that Luke, in bed eleven, would always be partially paralysed because of the disease which had invaded his brain, and that Jessica Brand, the most cheerful child of all, would not be alive next year. The children themselves would stop her from feeling too sad. Children had the greatest capacity to make the best of things, and could find enjoyment in situations where an adult would be miserable.

The morning flew, and she was still sitting on Timothy's bed, listening to his account of his operations, when Doreen appeared with the lunch-wagon.

'You still here, then?' Doreen asked her, as Penny moved off the bed and wheeled the boy's table over. 'Just about lunchtime, isn't it? Now you eat this all up today, young man,' she was saying, 'else you'll be skin and bone, and you'll slip down the plug-hole when you take a bath.'

Timothy seemed unalarmed at this terrible prospect, and only made a face at his food as she put the tray on his table.

''E eats 'ardly anything,' she remarked to Penny, shaking her head and returning to her trolley.

'Don't you feel like food, Timothy?' Penny asked.

Vigorously, Timothy shook his head, and made another face.

'Maybe if I sat here and talked to you, you could eat it and you wouldn't even notice. If I talked to you about something nice.'

'What?' he demanded.

'I'll tell you about my little brother who's learning to fly a helicopter.'

'Yeah?' Timothy's eyes widened.

'You have to stuff your dinner in while I tell you, thought,' she warned.

'Oh, yeah,' he said, deflated. He seemed to weigh it up. The idea of helicopters was too powerful.

'OK,' he conceded, and picked up his fork in readiness.

During the story of how Ted joined the navy and came to be flying helicopters, the boy kept up a fairly constant shovelling action. When he stopped, he found Penny stopped her story, except when his purpose in pausing was to ask a question.

In twenty minutes Timothy knew the story of young Ted Anderson's naval life, as well as all the details about helicopters which Penny could remember. And he had eaten his lunch for the first time in weeks. Penny was proud of her strategy.

Doreen, returning for the trays, seemed to regard it as a minor miracle. 'Well, will you look at that!' she exclaimed for half the ward to hear. 'Coaxing 'im for weeks, we've all been. And you get 'im to eat it all in one go. Blow me down!'

'Distraction's the name of the game. I'm an old hand at it. I've got eight brothers and sisters, you know, all younger than me.'

'Aha!' said Doreen. 'It's not some child psychology stuff you've got out of a book, then!'

Penny laughed. 'Hardly,' she confirmed.

Doreen appeared to be settling down to favour Penny with her opinion of the child psychology in books, but she quickly changed her mind when she saw the unit director walk into the ward.

'Oops. 'Ere comes 'is 'ighness,' she said, and scuttled off with the empty trays.

Penny got to her feet, afraid that Dr Adams would not approve of her sitting on patients' beds. He came to stand beside her, looking down at young Timothy from his impressive height.

'Eat your dinner, Master Preston?' he enquired.

'I ate it all,' Timothy stated defiantly.

Then Nicholas Adams surprised Penny and delighted his small patient by pretending speechless shock. 'You did?' he enquired faintly.

Timothy laughed, and nodded his head. 'She talked to me,' he explained, indicating Penny, and before Dr Adams could do more than shoot Penny a glance, continued, 'Do you think I can fly a helicopter when I'm big, Dr Nicholas?'

'Providing you eat your food and grow strong. I don't see any reason why not,' Dr Adams replied.

'Well, I will. But can she——' and, correctly interpreting the doctor's frown '—can Penny talk to me while I do?'

Nicholas Adams looked down at Penny briefly. 'I imagine Sister—er—Penny is going to be rather busy here, Timothy, but I'm sure she will talk with you whenever she can.'

'Of course I will, Timmy. I'll come every lunchtime,' promised Penny without hesitation.

Dr Adams tapped his fingers absently on the chart he was holding for a moment, as though thinking, then abruptly called to the sister who was passing.

'Sister Berensen, let's have a look at Timothy's head, shall we?'

'Certainly, Doctor,' said Berensen with a smile, and approached the bed.

Penny, feeling she had been dismissed, gave Timmy a wink and disappeared.

It was as well she had. Nurse Woods was looking for her to tell her that the parents of one of the new arrivals were here and might need someone to talk to. She dumped a file in Penny's hands and retreated with a call of, 'Good Luck.'

Penny glanced through the file. The child had fallen off a swing and fractured his skull. He had been operated on to relieve the pressure of the bleeding, and it was as yet uncertain how much damage had been done. This had been explained by the doctor, according to the notes. Penny guessed it was not medical advice they needed, but to talk about it.

She was right. The mother in the Quiet Room was crying, supported by a sad-looking husband who clearly didn't know what to do.

'She blames herself,' he said, after Penny had introduced herself.

'If only I hadn't left her for a moment,' the woman sobbed, and Penny sat down with an arm around her to begin the long task of talking it out and giving some comfort.

While Penny didn't make it to lunch that day, she was the topic of several lunchtime conversations. Among the wardsmaids and nurse-aides on one table, it was Doreen who introduced the topic, by relating how the new sister had persuaded Timmy to eat his lunch. 'A nice little thing' was the general verdict.

The description was rather different at the doctors' table. Here, her appearance seemed to weigh more heavily, again in her favour. The discussion was relatively unrestrained owing to the absence of any senior doctors, and she was pronounced all-in-all to be rather 'a stunner'.

'Stevenson seems to be making a bee-line for her already,' observed one of the interns. This remark caused some disgust. Larry Stevenson was evidently seen as stiff competition.

Penny would have been surprised to know that her name was being bandied about in yet higher circles. She was the topic of part of the conversation which passed between Drs Adams and Lewin over the cup of coffee which served them for lunch.

'Reserve judgement for a while, Nicholas, and you'll see I'm right,' Lewin was saying.

Adams sighed. 'I've no doubt we've needed a counsellor for a long time. It's only the priorities I'm doubtful about. In fact, I'm still convinced we've made a mistake. There's no point in having someone around who can look after the emotional needs of patients and parents, if we haven't sufficient staff to keep them alive.' There was a note of anger, now, in his voice.

Lewin dropped sugar into his cup, his face impassive.

'There's no point in arguing any further, I suppose,' said Adams with bitterness.

Lewin agreed. 'How are you finding her?' he asked, to deflect the discussion.

Adams was silent a moment. 'Very young, Oscar.' He shook his head. 'An older, more experienced person might have been better.'

'Hmm.' Lewin made a non-committal noise. 'She might surprise you.'

'Yes,' agreed Adams, with surprising venom in his voice. 'I might find she has an amazing knowledge of neurological medicine, and can step into the breach when half my doctors and nurses drop with exhaustion.'

Lewin took a deep breath. 'Your nurses would be less likely to drop with exhaustion if morale in the unit were higher, Nicholas.'

The remark angered Adams. 'Low morale is an occupational hazard in a department which deals with maimed and dying children, Doctor. If you don't like the way I run my unit——'

'Nicholas, Nicholas!' Lewin intervened. 'If I could have any surgeon in the world for that unit, I'd choose you. You know that. You're brilliant and dedicated.

But—you do tend to ignore the human side of the staff. Of yourself, for that matter.'

Adams played with his coffee-spoon, and stared unblinking and unresponsive at his cup.

By two o'clock, Penny had finished with the Robinsons, and was confident that the stricken mother was calmer and more able to cope than before. She was dismayed to bump into Dr Adams quite literally in the corridor, after seeing them off, knocking the files he was carrying to the floor. She bent down hurriedly to help him pick them up, her long dark hair falling over her face, and in her blindness managed to bump his head as well.

Penny was mortified. She held back her hair with one hand, scrambled for files with the other, and apologised at the same time, till Adams put a strong, well-shaped hand on her wrist to restrain her.

'Sister Anderson,' he said in a voice of resignation. 'Allow me to pick up the files before you inflict neurological damage on us both.'

Thoroughly embarrassed, she stole a look at his face. Neutral as his tone had been, she thought his face showed irritation. Guiltily she handed him the last file, and he took it with a brief 'Thank you', and was gone.

How to impress your boss on the second day of work! she thought, and found herself grinning despite her red face. At least he had remained polite, she reflected. You had to give him credit for that.

When Penny sat down that evening to have dinner with Carrie, she was more than ever certain that she was going to like her new job. She was glad that she had seen the advertisement and decided to apply. Her old job in the trauma section of Livingstone had been interesting enough, but it had lacked the day-to-day long-term contact with patients which this job offered. Penny had envied Carrie when she'd talked about the patients she had come to know well as the sister of a medical ward.

'Any nice doctors?' Carrie asked with a mischievous grin.

'One called Larry Stevenson,' said Penny.

'Oh, yes, the one who took you to see the boss.'

'He dropped in today while I was talking to one of the children—such a lovely child, Carrie, called Jessica. Big brown eyes and a really sweet disposition——'

'Yes, yes, but tell me what Larry looks like,' Carrie interrupted.'

'Oh—Larry,' Penny laughed. 'Well, reasonably tall, blond——'

'Good-looking?'

'Yes. Almost too good-looking,' she replied, consideringly.

'How can anyone be too good-looking?' Carrie asked.

'Well, I don't know. They're the sort of looks that don't really appeal to me. Too smooth, if you know what I mean.'

'Well, not really,' Carrie said, grinning. 'Sounds as if he likes you.'

'He hardly knows me!' Penny exclaimed. 'I'm quite willing to be friends, but I'm definitely not looking for romance. When it's ready, it'll come along all by itself, without my help. Right now, I'm more interested in getting settled down in my job.'

'I can't say I share your views on that topic, Penelope,' said Carrie severely. 'It always pays to keep a weather-eye out. I hope your father hasn't put you off the idea of falling in love.'

'Nonsense!' Penny laughed. 'He'd be only too happy for me to fall in love with a decent man.'

'He'd have to be dull, I suppose. What about the chief? All dedication and ideals, I take it. Aim high, I always say.' She was laughing.

'Oh, Carrie!' Penny protested. 'My father isn't dull at all. And as for the chief, you've got to be kidding. He's totally awesome.'

Carrie laughed. 'You always did find authority figures daunting, didn't you?'

'This one's more daunting than most,' Penny said fervently. 'And I just about knocked him over in the corridor today.'

Carrie laughed again. 'How did he take that?'

'Frostily polite, I'd have to say.'

'Oh, dear. He doesn't sound like much of a prospect.'

Penny readily agreed.

Penny spent the following morning with a number of children who were scheduled to go to Theatre. The theatres, recovery-rooms and wards were all on one floor of the large general hospital, a floor entirely devoted to children's neurology. She had not been to see the theatres until now, and they held an atmosphere of excitement for her. They were down one end of the building, and there were four of them.

Between the theatres and the recovery-rooms there was a wide rectangular vestibule with a desk for the medical secretary. It was here that the trolley-beds with their little patients on board were parked, before they were wheeled through the plastic swinging-doors to the theatres themselves.

In this room, Penny waited with several children who were drowsy from their pre-operative medication but still awake enough to be afraid. She had wondered at first whether she would be in the way there, but soon it transpired that the nursing staff were glad to have her relieve them of the task of comforting sick and frightened children while they sped about doing their other duties.

There was only one problem. One small child refused to let go of her hand when the time came to be wheeled into Theatre. And Penny, in ordinary clothes instead of sterile theatre garb, couldn't go in with him. He set up a bellow that echoed along the corridor, and all Penny's desperate endeavours couldn't persuade him to stop. Similarly, nothing short of force would make him let her go. Penny heartily wished herself anywhere else.

It was a sentiment which only increased when the surgeon appeared in the vestibule. It was the first time Penny had seen Dr Adams in his theatre gear. A green cap covered his hair and a surgical mask hung around his neck. He looked taller than ever in the surgical gown, and besides this he didn't look pleased.

Both Penny and the small boy quailed.

Adams took in the situation at a glance. His voice when he spoke was controlled enough but, for all that, his displeasure was obvious.

'No doubt you're trying to be helpful by being here, Sister Anderson. But you clearly haven't thought things through. Kindly be good enough to discuss any new ideas with me in future.'

Penny could only swallow hard and nod.

He turned then without another glance at her to the crying child, and spoke a few gentle words which miraculously quelled his wails.

'Have you ever seen an operating theatre?' he asked. 'It's a very interesting place. There's a great big light and a lot of wonderful machines. If you come with me, I'll show you.'

With Adams walking beside it, the porters wheeled the trolley through the plastic doors.

Penny escaped from the theatre section and stood by an open window in the corridor, gratefully letting a cool breeze play on her hot face.

She bit her lip. What a fool she'd been. She could hardly blame him for being annoyed. He'd probably had to scrub up again.

It had seemed such a good idea. They had seemed so afraid in the ward, the poor little things. It had seemed so simple to go up with them. It was true that she hadn't thought it through, and that she should have discussed it with someone.

All things considered, he had let her off quite lightly. He could have been a lot less polite than he had been. Ruefully Penny reflected how effective Nicholas Adams could make a reproof delivered with perfect politeness.

It was hard at first to talk unconcernedly to Timmy over his lunch, but after a while she forgot other things in telling him stories about her brothers. The strategy worked as well as it had on the preceding day, though Timothy shrewdly had already hit on the ploy of eating with laborious slowness to keep her there longer. Consequently, her own lunch-hour was almost over by the time they had finished their chat.

It was Berensen who brought the thought of the troubles in Theatre back to her.

'I hear you were the cause of an almighty fuss in Theatre this morning, Anderson,' she said, with what Penny could only think of as relish. 'Perhaps you ought to keep out of things that don't concern you.'

Penny was speechless, not because the remark was unjust, but because it was obviously so unkindly meant. But Berensen was continuing.

'And speaking of things that do concern you, Jessica Brand's parents are here. They want to talk to some-one about Jessica. I thought it might as well be you.'

It was hardly a flattering referral, but Penny was glad of it in any case, and only shocked to find, when she introduced herself to Mr and Mrs Brand, that they had been waiting for hours. At the end of the interview she was more than shocked—she was angry. Sister Berensen could easily have dealt with the query her-self. It would have taken her no more than five minutes.

As she walked down the corridor away from the Quiet Room, she thought to herself that it was going to be difficult to like Belinda Berensen. It didn't help her in the least to see Dr Adams striding towards her from the other direction. She knew an impulse to leap into a handy linen-room, but supposed that she must face him sooner or later. Penny prepared herself to make the apology she knew was due.

'Dr Adams,' she began unhappily, 'I'm sorry about this morning.'

He regarded her steadily with his clear grey eyes. 'Yes. You caused a considerable amount of trouble, didn't you? I don't like having innovation sprung upon me. Particularly ill-considered innovation. When you want to change the system in future, you'll discuss it with me.' His voice was stony.

Penny had blushed to the roots of her hair, but he might not have noticed. He was continuing, 'The idea, however, was a good one. It relieves the theatre staff of a task that they can well do without, and one which they're often not very good at. You can continue to come to Theatre, but in future put on theatre gear so you can come right in and avoid a repetition of this morning's fiasco.'

Penny no longer knew what to feel. He actually liked her idea! He wanted to put it into practice. She should feel pleased about that. But such was the force of his first reproof, however politely worded, that she couldn't quite manage pleasure. She had to make do with feeling a little better than before, and with vowing that from now on she was going to keep a very low profile as far as the boss was concerned.

She had to admit to herself, however, sitting in her office later, that he had been fair. Some people would have rejected the whole idea without further thought. He hadn't done that. Fairness was an important attribute in a boss, she told herself. It was more important than friendliness.

Nevertheless, when Larry stopped by to say hello later, Penny found herself grateful for a little friendliness. He asked her to dinner the following evening and, though a warning bell went off in her head, his good humour was so pleasant that she ignored it and accepted.

Penny only wondered whether she had done the right thing in accepting when she accompanied a child into the theatre where he was working next morning.

Behind the scrub-sister's back, he threw her a kiss and winked. Penny hoped it was only a boyish joke. The last thing she wanted was for Larry to become amorous. She made up her mind to let him know that she was quite uninterested in romance, and succeeded in the end at reconciling herself to their dinner-date by telling herself that it was the perfect opportunity for such a confidence.

Her happy mood returned when, back in the ward with Timothy, Doreen brought in two lunch-trays instead of one.

Not that the sight of the other tray did much to delight young Timothy.

'I don't have to eat two, do I?' he demanded in dismay.

'Course not,' said Doreen. 'This one for Penny.'

'Oh, thank you, Doreen!' Penny cried, touched at the woman's evident thoughtfulness.

'Don't thank me,' said the lady. 'Not but what I thought it was a shame for you to miss your lunch. But I don't have the power to order extra dinners.'

'Was it Sister Berensen?' Penny asked, thinking it might be a gesture designed to bury the hatchet.

''Er?' snorted Doreen. 'Ha! Catch 'er ladyship thinking of anyone else but 'erself and 'er precious Dr Big Chief—not that I've really got anything to say against 'im. And actually it was 'im got you this extra lunch sent up. Sez you're to 'ave one till you stop spending most of your lunch-hour with Timothy.'

Penny could think of nothing to say, but 'Oh!' in a wondering way, and presently Doreen pushed the traymobile on to the next bed. Penny was touched and grateful at her boss's consideration, but, more than anything, surprised. Only yesterday she'd caused him considerable nuisance, and he had made no effort to hide his disapproval. The eyes that had held hers in the corridor had been cold and uncompromising. And yet today he was concerned that she managed to get some lunch.

Penny thought about it as she fed Tim. She thought perhaps she saw how it was. He ran a tight ship here. He expected a lot from himself and his staff, but he was basically fair-minded and decent. Penny had met others like him. Once you got to know them, often you found you liked them. Perhaps under the austere exterior there was a warm and caring human being. Struggling to get out, thought Penny, and found herself grinning at the image it raised.

CHAPTER THREE

AT THE end of the day, when the wardsmaids were beginning to wheel the teas around, Penny left the ward to play a game of tennis on the hospital courts with a friend who worked in another department. She had chosen this way to fill in the time till Larry would be off and ready to go to dinner, rather than have him pick her up at home.

Somehow she didn't wish for Larry to come to her home. She supposed it was part of her wish to keep him at a distance. Not that there was, in all probability, any need for that, she told herself. She was being insufferably conceited in thinking that his friendliness amounted to anything.

With these thoughts she showered and changed after the game, and walked over to the main foyer of the hospital where they had arranged to meet. He was there already, and looked pleased when he saw her, coming to take her arm.

'You look lovely, Penelope,' he said, and embarrassed her by bestowing a kiss on her forehead. Maybe she had been right after all. . .

She had been right. It became speedily apparent, over dinner, that Larry was inclined to be romantic. Penny wondered how she could possibly put a stop to his exaggerated compliments and over-zealous admiration without seeming churlish and petty.

As the coffee and liqueurs came, it became necessary to take a stand. He had taken her hand and kissed it.

'Larry,' she began, and he looked up at her with smiling eyes. He certainly was attractive.

'Yes, my Penelope?'

Penny could think of no subtle way to say it.

'Larry, don't get romantic,' she said with a pleading note in her voice. 'I'd like to be friends, but. . .'

He smiled at her softly, but held on to her hand.

'Ah, I've rushed you,' he said theatrically.

'You could say that!' laughed Penny. 'I've known you two days! And besides, I'm not ready for romance for some time yet.'

Her tone was decided, and with an air of sadness he put her hand down on the table and patted it.

'Ah, well,' he said. 'Then I'll be Larry the faithful friend, the staunch protector and stalwart guide until that wonderful day in the future when the scales fall from your beautiful eyes and——'

'Enough!' cried Penny, laughing. 'OK, I've got the idea. We both have. Let's talk about something else.'

'The feasibility of love at first sight?' he suggested.

'No!' she cried with vehemence.

Penny steadfastly refused all Larry's offers of a lift, and caught the bus home after dinner. She didn't mind doing it. It was a very short bus-ride to her home, and at least it kept Larry a little remote. He was very nice, she thought, but she did not see that she could ever feel romantic about him.

Several days passed quickly at work. Penny found three was a lot for her to do. Reassuring the children

and their parents, sometimes helping them to express
their grief, and giving practical aid to poor parents
who could ill afford the frequent trips to the hospital
more than filled her days. A couple of times she stayed
late, because her work was simply not done. It didn't
matter to Penny—she was loving it. On both these
occasions she met Dr Adams, prowling the wards to
check on the children, and looking as though he had
no thought of going home.

She wondered when he did go home, and what
home was like. Penny could not imagine him outside
the hospital environment and out of his hospital coat.
She knew from the grapevine that he wasn't married,
but was there a lady waiting for him at home? She
would have to be patient, that was for sure.

Dr Adams had seen her where she sat at the bedside
of five-year-old Lindy. He paused, arrested in the act
of striding down the ward, and slowly approached the
bed. He looked at Penny for a moment, and then at
Lindy who had just closed her eyes to go to sleep, the
tear-stains still upon her little face.

Penny wondered whether he was going to say anything at all. He was standing at the foot of the bed, tall
and dark with big, well-sculptured hands upon the rail.
Penny hadn't noticed his hands before.

But finally he spoke.

'Don't sacrifice yourself to this job, Sister
Anderson.'

It was spoken lightly; it may even have been ironi-
cally. Penny couldn't tell from his tone. She looked up
to encounter grey eyes gazing on her with an
expression equally indecipherable. Penny felt a sudden
tension seize her. Her heart speeded up. It was an odd

feeling. There was no doubt about it, she thought—
she found her boss unnerving. Quickly, she looked
away, and groped for an answer.

'N-no, Dr Adams,' she managed to say, but added
softly because it was true, 'it couldn't ever be that. I
love it.'

Penny had thought he would make a brief comment
and go. He didn't. Instead he sat down in the other
chair, and she felt him resume his scrutiny.

'Do you?' he asked at last, and it made her glance
up. His face was turned to her, his look searching.

'Yes,' she said. 'It's not like—like work.' She
thought it sounded silly, but when she looked back at
him she thought his lips had curved a little—just a
relaxation of their normal line. The embryo of a smile?
she wondered.

There was another pause. Then, 'Do you have a
family?' he asked abruptly. 'A—someone at home?'

'I live with a girlfriend,' she told him. 'I learned to
nurse with her. We're very good at putting each other's
dinner in the oven.'

She heard him make the briefest noise of understanding. And she found herself wondering how he
survived, given the hours he put in at the hospital.
Before she could think too much, she asked, 'Do you
have a family, Dr Adams?'

He didn't sound annoyed at the question. His tone
was neutral when he answered.

'No. I have an excellent housekeeper who comes in
to cook, and after a great struggle I've mastered the
reheat control on the microwave.'

Penny gave a spurt of laughter. She couldn't help it.
It was so comic to think of a man like him struggling

with something so simple. She glanced up at him quickly, hoping it hadn't offended him. But it was all right, she thought. His face even held a look of faint humour, which Penny liked.

And his next remark was made in a dry tone.

'I suppose you find that sort of thing easy?'

She found herself beginning to grin. 'Well. . .' she began, and found she could think of nothing diplomatic to say.

'Yes,' he completed for her. Then, in another moment, he had risen to his feet. 'Don't stay too late,' he said brusquely. 'You'll become very tired.'

Penny felt a flash of gratitude for his concern. And that reminded her of those lunches. She had yet to thank him.

'Dr Adams,' she said quickly, as he stepped away, 'thank you for arranging my lunch.'

He paused the briefest moment. 'You can't work well without adequate nutrition,' he said shortly, and walked away.

Penny felt afterwards that she had been right in her earlier thoughts. He was a man who pushed himself hard, and who demanded high standards of others. But he was not without human concern for them. Given time she thought she may come to like him. Whether she could ever feel at ease with him was another matter. He wasn't entirely devoid of a sense of humour, she thought, and that helped. Even so, it made him only marginally less daunting.

Friday was a day for meetings, she found. There was the hospital social workers' meeting and the children's neuro unit meeting to attend. Generally, Penny detested meetings. Compared to actually working with the patients, they were dull. In this hospital, however, where she worked virtually independently of anyone else, she felt glad to go to the social workers' meeting, and hoped to receive support and advice.

In some measure, she did. The senior social worker of the hospital willingly gave her opinion on some of Penny's cases, and regretted that Penny had to work so much alone. She was a motherly type, with a deep concern for people, and also a woman of vast experience.

'You must come and consult me whenever you feel the need to, Penny,' she said. 'It's a difficult ward you're on, in one way and another. Don't hesitate to bring your troubles here and enlist our help.'

Penny was grateful, and thanked Miss Durham sincerely. She hoped she would not have too many 'troubles' to bother the lady with. It was clear from the rest of the discussion that the senior social worker was a very busy woman.

The unit meeting was next, and Penny was late for it, by virtue of being stopped on her way by the parents of little Jessie Brand. They only wanted to say hello, apparently, and quickly let her go when she told them she had a meeting to attend. But she wondered whether there was something on the mother's mind. She had a vague air of agitation, and Penny had noticed that as they'd spoken she'd twisted her fingers nervously in front of her.

But there was no time to consider it now. Penny glanced at the clock in the corridor as she flew along, and saw that she was already five minutes behind. She hated to be late for meetings, and wondered whether everyone would turn to look at her as she endeavoured to slip in unnoticed.

Mercifully, most of the occupants of the meeting-room did not pay her too much attention. Dr Adams silently noted her tardy arrival, however, and Penny became only too conscious that she was flushed and breathless from running, and that her hair was all over the place. She was thankful that his only reaction was to look at her.

They were discussing her little friend, Timothy. New scans had been taken of his head, and these were now on the lighted screens at the front of the room. It seemed he was not recovering as fast as the doctors had expected. The scans offered no explanation. Clini-cally, it seemed, the boy should be ready for discharge. But all who had seen the boy, listlessly lying in his bed, pushing his food about with a half-hearted air and complaining about feeling sick, could not be happy that he had made a complete recovery.

'I can't find anything clinically wrong with him,' Dr Adams was saying. 'I think it may be best if we discharge him. He may do much better at home. Perhaps he's simply pining here.'

Penny sat tensely in her chair. She wondered if she should give her own opinion. She was a very new and very junior member of this staff, and as such would be expected to sit quietly and say nothing, she was sure. But over her last lunchtimes spent with Timmy, she had begun to think that something indeed was wrong. Quite why she believed it, she would not have been able to say; but she had come to think that Timmy did not want to go home.

Oh, dear, she thought. Will I say it? It might seem

that I'm interfering, or thinking rather highly of my own opinion. But what about poor Timmy? Should he suffer for my cowardice? It was the deciding factor.

'Dr Adams,' Penny said in a small voice, and he turned to her, his face expressionless and waiting. 'I've wondered a little in the past few days whether Timothy *wants* to go home.'

He raised an eyebrow in silence, and she went on, a little unhappily, 'It's nothing I can put my finger on, unfortunately, but I just wonder if there's some trouble. . .' Her voice trailed away.

Adams considered a moment. 'We certainly get children here from bad family backgrounds,' he said at length. 'But generally even they want to go home. And this boy is not one of them. He has a good home and is the only child of what appear to be extremely doting parents. Have you any evidence for your opinion?'

Penny blushed. She had no evidence at all. And she realised just what spectre her words must call up in all their minds. A child who didn't want to go home always raised the suspicion of child abuse.

Penny shook her head. 'No,' she admitted uncomfortably. 'And I'm not accusing his parents of anything. I—agree with you about them. It's something else,' she finished lamely.

Adams spoke curtly. 'In view of the fact that statements like yours do raise suspicion, I think you should be very careful in making them. You had better explore your impressions a little more carefully, Sister Anderson.'

Penny felt humiliated. He was right, of course, but she couldn't help feeling he was unnecessarily severe.

She could see that Larry was torn between sympathy for her and anger at Nicholas Adams. It didn't make her feel better.

She was glad when the meeting ended, and since it was lunchtime she went off to talk to Timothy and, indeed, to 'explore her impressions further'.

Timmy obviously envied Penny her large family. She was sure it was lonely for him, being an only child, but she wondered whether there was more to it than that. She tried to get him to talk about it, giving him gentle leads. It was when he said that he wished he had a big brother, that things began to come clear.

'What would it be like if you had a big brother?' she asked.

'He'd do things with me,' said Timmy. 'And—he'd look after me.'

'Your mummy and daddy look after you, don't they, Timmy?' she probed.

'Yeah,' he said, and Penny could hear the note of misery.

'Do they do things with you?'

'Yeah,' he said. 'Mummy. Daddy goes to work.'

'What does your mummy do with you?' she asked.

'Oh, plays and things. She reads me stories. An' she helped me make a dinosaur. . .'

For a moment Penny thought he was going to cheer up and tell her about the dinosaur, but instead his voice trailed away and he stopped.

'What's the matter?' she asked him gently, and suddenly he began to cry.

'She's going away,' he sobbed. 'I heard them. She said she's going away when I'm better. I don't wanna be better. Not ever, ever, ever!'

Penny held the little boy as he cried, and he clung to her, sobbing and heart-brokenly repeating the words 'not ever, not ever, not ever.'

It was late afternoon when Penny had finished on the ward and could sit down to write a report on Timmy. She had wondered at first whether she should tell Dr Adams about it straight away, but she thought a written report would do just as well, and then she wouldn't have to see him. So she wrote it all out in the notes, and asked for permission at the bottom for a special meeting with Timothy's parents. She took it and left it with Miss Fosdyke for Dr Adams, and returned to the office they had given her to catch up on the reports that had not got done.

Penny was surprised to see that it was six o'clock when a knock on her door made her look up. Her 'come in' brought the unit director into the room.

'I saw the light under your door,' he said. 'Had I known you were still here I would have come and spoken to you about this earlier.' Timmy's file was in his hand. He regarded her for a moment. 'Working late again, Sister Anderson?'

Penny blushed at his scrutiny. 'There w-were too many meetings today,' she stammered.

She wondered immediately whether that had sounded critical, and was further unnerved when he continued to face her expectantly.

'Are you afraid my weight will be too much for the furniture?' he asked at length. 'Or may I sit down?'

'I'm s-sorry,' she blurted. 'I s-sort of thought you would if you wanted to.'

He raised one eyebrow and, for the very first time, Penny saw a faint but definite smile lift the corners of his mouth. She could only think that she had been right on that very first day. Nicholas Adams, smiling, was a very handsome man.

'Please sit down, Dr Adams,' she managed, and he suited his action to her words, leaning back in the chair with his long legs stretched out before him.

His face was serious again. 'I've read your report.'

Penny was unaccountably anxious. How would he take her having been right?

Then, for the second time, a slow smile relaxed his face, and he said softly, 'Well done, Sister.'

The words of praise brought the colour afresh to her face, and she couldn't immediately think what to say. But it didn't matter. He hadn't finished.

'I'm sorry if I sounded severe in the meeting.'

Penny began to shake her head, to tell him she understood, but he interrupted.

'No, I want you to understand. Child abuse is a sensitive topic here. The nursing staff feel very strongly about parents who abuse their children. If we had left any idea in their minds at all that that was why Tim didn't want to go home, then I'm afraid their attitudes might have changed towards the parents. I didn't want that to happen.'

'I shouldn't think you'd want it to happen even if they were child-abusers,' suggested Penny tentatively. 'It's not very helpful for the nursing staff to punish people who need help.'

He looked at her thoughtfully. 'I agree with you. But I also understand how they feel. They are the ones who care for the children. It's bad enough when a child has accidental injuries. When they're not accidental. . . I don't condone their attitude or encourage it, but I do understand it.'

Slowly, Penny nodded her head. Nicholas Adams had a difficult job here. He must be rather lonely, she thought suddenly. His general demeanour would not invite friendly gestures from his staff. He seemed to have run out of things to say, and sat playing absently with Penny's stapler. At length he put it down, and got up to go.

'Well, I certainly agree with you about the need to speak to Timothy's parents, Penny. Feel free to arrange a meeting.'

It was the first time he had used her first name. It made him sound so much more human. Once again when he had gone, Penny was forced to admit that while Nicholas Adams might at times be rather formidable, he also strove to be fair. He gave praise where he felt it was due.

And if he continued to smile occasionally, it would help a great deal.

It was rather late to go home and cook her tea. Penny decided instead to have tea in the hospital dining-room, and she joined Larry willingly enough when he saw her there and called her over.

'What are you doing here so late?' he asked with a smile. 'No home to go to?'

'Just too much to do,' she replied.

'Nick driving you into the ground?' His handsome face took on a scowl. 'He shouldn't have put you down like that in the meeting.'

'It's all right, Larry. I understand why he did it. He came and explained, actually.'

Larry raised his eyebrows.

'I was right about Timmy, you see.' She explained what had happened. 'So, you see, he gives credit where he thinks it's due, Larry. I don't think he's so bad.'

'I see.' He played with the salt cellar with an enigmatic smile. 'Well, you're probably right,' he said, 'as long as you're capable of functioning like an infallible machine. I'm afraid I'm rather human.'

'I don't know about that either, Larry,' she said, and she told him about the lunches Nicholas Adams had ordered for her.

Larry raised his eyebrows and smiled rather a wry smile. 'I see,' he said slowly. 'But this is very interesting. Can our leader have finally discovered the vestiges of human emotion in himself?'

'What do you mean?' she asked, frowning.

Larry smiled. 'My dear little lamb, you are adorable, you know.'

Penny blushed, as the meaning of his words sank in. 'Rubbish!' she cried. 'Sister Berensen has been after him for ages, I'm told, and she's much more attractive than I am.'

Larry laughed. 'If you weren't getting so heated I'd argue with you about that.'

'Well, I am. So don't,' she retorted crossly.

'I'm sorry,' he said, and sounded quite contrite. 'I won't suggest such a thing again. But Penny, I must say this. Don't delude yourself about Nicholas Adams. I'll agree with you that he can be quite charming at times, but he's also capable of being utterly ruthless. He is dedicated to his work. It's the only thing that matters to him. And if you get in the way he's quite capable of turning on you. You're such a soft-hearted little thing. I don't want to see you hurt.'

'I won't get hurt, and I won't delude myself. About

anyone,' she said with emphasis. 'I just don't think he's so bad, that's all.'

Larry sighed. 'I hope he doesn't give you any reason to change your mind,' he said.

Penny caught the bus home, still thinking of the two conversations she had held tonight. Larry really resented his boss. She supposed that it wasn't unusual among junior doctors, particularly when their superiors were so clearly that—superior. He had said some silly things, she thought. There was no way that Nicholas Adams would ever be interested in her. He hardly even seemed to notice the glamorous Sister Berensen. And as for her, she doubted whether she would ever overcome her diffidence enough to feel anything but nervousness in his presence.

CHAPTER FOUR

THINGS seemed to speed up in the children's neuro unit over the next few weeks. Penny learned that she had come in a period of relative quiet, and that the normal pace of the unit was more like the one the staff were suffering under now.

She began to feel the force of Dr Adams' earlier assertion that they needed more nursing and medical staff. In Theatre and in the ward, things were frenetic. It seemed that cases came in faster than the beleaguered staff could possibly handle them. Yet somehow they did.

How much of this was due to the fact that the nursing staff consistently worked hours of overtime, and the doctors round the clock, Penny could plainly see. What she could not see was how a unit could possibly function competently at this alarming pace for any length of time. She helped them as much as she could, taking over as many tasks as she could from the nurses, and fitting in her own work around them.

Once again she found herself changing dressings, bathing children and giving pain-killers just as she had as a general nurse. It didn't help that her own work expanded with the influx of customers. They had had some very serious trauma cases along with new cases of tumour, meningitis, encephalitis. Commonly Penny found herself still counselling grief-stricken parents at eight o'clock at night.

48

It wasn't so bad for her, she thought. She didn't actually have responsibility for the patients' lives and well-being. She didn't have on her mind the thought that one mistake, born of panic or fatigue, could have disastrous consequences.

After some weeks, during which the pressure did not seem to let up, it was apparent to Penny that the nurses, at least, were feeling the strain. She guessed, from the comments of the latter, that the doctors were faring no better, though she had hardly seen them. She only caught a glimpse of one or other of them when she brought a child down to Theatre, and then it was obvious that they had no time to say hello.

This morning it seemed to her that Theatre was bedlam. Organised chaos might have been closer to the mark, but Penny was not too sure. She waited with a child, a little boy, who had been given his premedication four hours ago but who looked like having to have it again, so long was the wait for the theatre. Two other cases had already been rescheduled, and everyone prayed that no emergencies would crop up.

Sister Jenkins had finally come out to say they were finishing up, and she paused gratefully at Penny's side for her first five-minute break since seven o'clock.

Penny smiled at her, and she grinned back wryly.

'How's it going?' asked Penny.

Jenkins raised her eyes to heaven. 'Dreadful,' she said flatly. 'My nurses are slow-witted with fatigue, and the boss is growing more like a thunder-cloud each minute. He's been up all night, and God knows how much sleep he got the night before, and we're just waiting for someone to drop something. Then the storm'll break!'

'Heavens!' said Penny. 'That mustn't help.'

'It doesn't,' replied Jenkins. 'But you can hardly blame him. He takes the brunt of the strain.'

Another nurse had come out of the theatre to join them. 'They're just cleaning up,' she said. 'It went pretty well, didn't it? The op, I mean, not the atmosphere. Nick's just phoned the maintenance staff and told them to get him a theatre clock that doesn't tick.'

They stared at one another for a moment, then burst into laughter. It seemed so comic.

'Good Lord!' gasped Jenkins. 'He's cracking up!'

'I don't see why he shouldn't,' returned the other nurse.

'Sister Jenkins,' Penny put in, 'I don't know if anyone's told you, but Jerome here had his premedication at least four hours ago.'

Jenkins swore under her breath. 'Better get on to it before all hell breaks loose. Thanks, Penny. You're a gem.'

In a short time the team in Theatre were ready for Jerome. It was too short a time, really. His second lot of pre-op pills had not had time to settle him down again, and he clung to Penny as they wheeled him in, and cried bitterly.

But Penny was dressed in theatre garb and she walked in beside him. She was the one familiar and comforting thing in an alien and frightening place for the small boy. He refused to let go of her.

He also refused to lie still while the anaesthetist gave him his anaesthetic, and Penny had to work hard to calm him down and convince him that all was OK. Finally he let them give him the injection, and Penny had time to dart a glance at Adams before she left the theatre.

His eyes met hers over his mask for a moment, and Penny felt a shock run through her. She tried to smile at him politely, but she was too struck by the paleness of his face and the strain which was written there.

And in another moment he had turned away.

Penny had occasion to see the boss again in the afternoon, and he didn't look any better. She had returned to Theatre to see whether she might be able to exchange a word with him between cases. There were some parents for her to see, and she needed information that only Nicholas Adams could give.

He stood in the doorway of the first anaesthetic bay, speaking to the anaesthetist, as Penny made her tentative approach.

'Want me?' he asked briefly, glancing down at her.

Penny nodded, and looked apologetic.

'Ten minutes, then?' he called to the anaesthetist, and a voice answered, 'Make it twelve.'

Adams turned to Penny. 'Problem?' he asked.

She shook her head hastily. 'Not really. Just information.'

He gave a short sigh. 'Thank God for that,' he said, and surprised her by taking her arm and steering her into the common-room. 'I need fluid,' he explained. 'Sit down.'

It took Penny a moment to recover from the novel sensation of being touched by him. For a few seconds she could still feel the firm grip of his hand on her bare upper arm.

She stood for a moment, collecting herself, then said quickly, 'I'll make it. You sit down.'

He paused and glanced at her, and she blushed furiously, thinking she had made it sound like an order, but he only nodded, said 'Thanks,' and lowered himself gratefully into a chair.

Penny put a cup under the spout of the coffee-machine, and was concerned to realise that her hands were trembling. What an idiot she was! There was no need to be as frightened of him as that. He'd only taken her arm. Penny shook her head at herself, and concentrated on making his coffee.

She noticed some scones on the table, left-overs from the others' afternoon tea, and put three on a saucer and brought them to him with his coffee. Her hand still shook as she handed him the cup, and a little coffee sloshed over into the saucer.

He put it on the table in front of him, reached out a hand, and caught her again by the wrist.

'What is it?' he demanded. 'Are you worried about something?' His grey eyes searched her face.

She forced herself to speak, though her tongue suddenly seemed glued to the roof of her mouth, and the room much too hot. 'No! No,' she gasped. 'Nothing. I'm—I'm just clumsy. I'm sorry.'

He watched her through narrowed eyes a moment longer, then slowly released his grasp. 'Sit down and tell me what you want to know,' he said at last.

It didn't take long for him to give her the information she needed. And it was only a short time later that she stood in her office, gazing sightlessly out over the gardens, and wondering what on earth about him shook her so. She had always been nervous with those in command, but she couldn't remember being this bad before.

Unconsciously, Penny rubbed the place on her arm where his hand had been.

In the morning Penny learned that a full night's sleep had been denied Dr Adams once again. Shortly after one o'clock he had been called out to look at a child who seemed to be sinking fast and without reason.

The child was still with them this morning, and was apparently picking up.

Penny didn't learn exactly what had happened, but she did learn that there had been a more serious row than usual between Adams and Dr Stevenson.

She heard variously throughut the morning that Larry was a 'slacker' and Adams a 'slave-driver', but very few people seemed to know exactly what had gone on.

It was very bad for morale, Penny reflected. And the Lord knew, if there was one thing they needed now, it was morale. The day passed as busily as the one before, and Penny was glad she was not called upon to go to Theatre.

Today's cases were a cheerful lad of twelve who didn't need to hold her hand, and a car-accident victim who wouldn't have known if she had. His surgery took many hours, and was unsuccessful. He died shortly after. Penny could not help but think it was just as well. Surely he would have been terribly disabled.

She wondered how Nicholas Adams and Larry felt, working on the child hour after hour, and knowing the fate they may be condemning him to if they saved him.

There must be times, she reflected, when they repented of the Hippocratic oath.

Penny's main source of anxiety that day was Jessica Brand. Jessica was a twelve-year-old child with large brown eyes and a sweet nature to match. She was a long-term patient of the ward, and would probably stay there now till she died. Home was a station in the far-west of New South Wales, and Jessica had not seen it since she had come to the city for investigation. She wore a brown wig at the moment to cover the straggly regrowth of hair where they had shaved it for her surgery.

The surgery had been to no avail. Jessica's tumour was malignant and, although the removal of part of it had given her an extra few months of life, it could not save her.

Jessie was proud of her status as 'old lady' of the ward. Not that she was the oldest child there, but she had been there the longest. She loved to help the new kids settle in, and she would comfort them when they missed their homes, and try to occupy them when they were bored. The nurses loved her, not only because she helped them, but because she was a lovely child— gentle and loving and good. After a month it was Penny that Jessica loved best. Penny put it down to the fact that she had more time to talk with Jessie, but the nurses could see it was not only that. Jessica had an admiration and trust in Penny that was very special, and Penny loved her in return.

But it seemed to Penny recently, and especially today, that Jessie was somehow different from before. She looked forlorn and anxious, and her little face seemed paler than usual. Penny wondered whether she was worried about something, or whether she felt ill.

'Are you all right, Jessie?' she had asked.

'I'm just a little tired today. That's all,' the child had answered.

Penny could not press her, but neither could she be content. She wondered whether she ought to ask Dr Adams to look at the girl, or whether she would be adding to his work for no good reason.

She pondered on it. She could always ask Larry. He wasn't as busy as the boss. Penny frowned to herself. Somehow she didn't want to do that. She had to admit to herself that she wanted Adams himself to look at her. Jess was her special patient and somehow Larry wouldn't do.

Her reverie was rudely interrupted by Sister Berensen.

'I don't know what you're standing around dreaming for, Andersen,' she snapped as she came into the kitchen, 'but if you've got nothing to do you could go and dress that kid who's going home.'

Penny, practising what her father preached, agreed to go and do it, as sweetly as she could. But Berensen, she decided, certainly got her goat.

She wasn't good enough for Dr Adams, Penny decided, then wondered at the thought.

As she went to dress the child, Penny noticed another of their young patients crying miserably. Penny went to see what she could do.

'Lisa,' she called. 'Lisa, what's the matter?'

The little girl rubbed her head with her hand and continued to cry.

'Is your head hurting, Lisa?'

Lisa nodded miserably.

Penny frowned. The child was having regular analgesics. She picked up her medication chart to see when Lisa had had the last lot and whether she was due for more. What she saw surprised her. Lisa hadn't been given anything at all since early morning. Penny sighed. 'I'll get you a tablet to take the pain away, Lisa. It won't be long.'

Penny found Sister Berensen writing up notes at the desk. 'If it's all right, Sister Berensen, I'll give Lisa her tablet. She seems to have missed a dose.'

Penny was afraid that Berensen would feel she was interfering, though she had helped with the drugs before. But the blonde sister seemed too busy to care.

'Suit yourself, Anderson,' she said. 'You're a trained nurse. I haven't got time to be everywhere.'

It seemed the ward staff were feeling the strain as well.

Penny's chance to talk to Dr Adams about Jess came that afternoon, when he came to the ward after Theatre. She was sorry to have to trouble him. He looked, if anything, worse than he had the previous day. And she couldn't explain very adequately what she was worried about.

He frowned at her. 'What are you saying?' he demanded curtly.

'Just that she seems much more tired,' was all she could reply, and she heard him sigh, perhaps in exasperation.

'I'll look at her,' he said abruptly.

She wanted to say she was sorry, that she realised how tired he must be. But his face didn't invite further conversation and, in any case, Larry had come to claim her for their second dinner together, which she had agreed to on the basis of his promise to behave like a friend.

'Ready for that cannelloni?' he asked her cheerfully.

She nodded and picked up her bag, feeling rather guilty that they were leaving Adams here to finish the work. It was a feeling accentuated when she noticed his gaze on them. It held, she thought, a look of contempt. It might have been meant for Larry, or for her. Or maybe it had encompassed them both.

True to his promise, Larry behaved as a friend at dinner.

In fact, Penny thought, he was rather subdued. He wore his usual air of gaiety, but somehow it didn't ring true.

'I suppose you heard about my little fracas with Nick?' he said at length.

His tone was light, but Penny thought he looked unhappy.

'A little,' she said. 'Not enough to know what happened.'

Larry gave a wry smile. 'I suppose I should be glad about that, anyway.' He played absently with the salt cellar. 'The fact of the matter is that I'm not like our boss. I'm very human, I'm afraid.'

He looked up at her, and there was almost an appeal in his face.

'Most of us are,' she said gently, and smiled.

Larry's face relaxed a little. 'Bless you, my lovely friend. You have such a sympathetic face, do you know that? I'm not surprised you're a hit with the kids. The thing is, Penny, he makes no allowances at all. No allowance for inexperience, for fatigue, for anything. . .' His voice was bitter. 'I don't have his experience. I don't know what he knows. Sometimes I make mistakes.'

'We all do,' said Penny softly.

Larry shook his head. 'No. No, Nick doesn't make mistakes. That's what makes it so hard to work with him. He doesn't make mistakes, and he can't accept it when others do. That's what makes me hate him. . .'

Penny felt sorry for him. And yet she felt he didn't understand Nicholas Adams. She tried to find the words to tell him what she thought.

'Larry, maybe it's just his way of—of encouraging you to do the best you can possibly do.'

Larry's eyes held a cynical light. But he didn't argue. He patted her hand.

'Maybe it is, little friend,' he said. 'And, in any case, I shouldn't be troubling you with it. Forget it. Let's have another glass of that excellent wine.'

The following morning she found Dr Adams had kept his promise with Jess. He had seen her that very night.

'What did he do?' asked Penny.

'Oh, prodded and poked,' grinned Jessie. 'And listened with his stethoscope—for hours, and took my blood pressure, and asked me a million questions, and got me to do funny things. He's so nice, Penny. I love Dr Nicholas. As much as I love you, almost.'

Penny's heart gave a twinge and she squeezed Jessie's hand. It was not the first time she'd heard such things of Dr Adams. He might be distant and severe with his staff, but there was no doubt he was loved by the children. It was another reason for thinking Larry was wrong about the boss. No man whom so many children loved could be as unfeeling as Larry thought he was. He was just so overworked. . . .

She wondered what he had found with Jess, and whether she would see him today to ask him. But it proved unnecessary. When she reached her office, she found a note slid under the door. It was brief.

'No apparent physical cause.'

This was all it said, and it was signed with his scribbled initials.

Well, that was good for Jess, anyway, even if it meant she'd been wasting Dr Adams' time. If it was nothing physical, it could be resolved.

There was another note on her desk. One of the sisters, asking her if she had some time to spend with Jessie's parents. It was just what Penny wanted to do.

They were waiting in the Quiet Room when she got there, and they looked worried. Mr and Mrs Brand greeted Penny like an old friend, and with a certain measure of relief, she thought.

Penny came to the point as soon as she could.

'Mrs Brand, something is troubling you, I think,' she said gently. 'Would you like to tell me about it?'

The lady looked glad, but she hesitated, seeming not to know how to put it. At last it came out in a rush.

'Oh, Penny,' she said, her eyes filling with tears. 'We don't know what to do. What to tell Jessie. She usually doesn't speak of the future at all, but lately—she's been asking us about when she can come home, and, and—I keep telling her lies.'

The woman began to sob, and her husband tried to comfort her.

'Steady on, Ellen,' he was saying. 'Don't blame yourself. What else can you do? You can't tell a little girl she's—she's never going to. . .' His voice trailed away.

Penny took a breath. 'I think you're wrong, Mr Brand,' she said, and they both looked up at her, startled. 'I think you can tell her, and that you must. You see, I think Jessie knows you're lying to her. I think Jessie wants to know the truth, and that she is strong enough to cope with it.'

The parents looked from one to the other, and back to Penny.

'I just couldn't,' the mother said brokenly.

'Would you like me to talk to her?' asked Penny, aware as she did so that she was volunteering for a very painful task. 'I've noticed that she's troubled. If it's this that is troubling her, then it's best for me to answer her questions truthfully, and help her to accept it.'

The mother was crying again, but she sounded grateful when she said, 'Oh, yes, Penny. I had been so hoping that someone would help us.'

Penny went back to the ward with the intention of speaking to Jessie straight away.

They had taken her to the day-room, a sunny apartment that looked out on to the sprawling hospital grounds, ten floors below them. It was at the far end of the ward, adjacent to the theatres, and a dozen youngsters were there this morning, some sitting in chairs, and others in their beds.

Penny knew that she needed privacy for this talk

with Jessie, and she went to see if the little office off the theatres, where senior doctors sometimes briefed interns, was free. She was sure it would be. Theatre would be in full swing at this hour.

She was wrong. The door to the office was ajar, but it was not empty. It was, in fact, occupied by a young nurse in theatre garb, who had thrown her cap on the floor and who was sitting in a chair with her head on the desk, sobbing as though her heart would break.

Penny hesitated, and then reflected that it was surely her job to give what support she could to the staff as well as the patients. She took a few tentative paces towards the girl, and the nurse looked up, startled. Penny hadn't seen her before.

'Hello,' said Penny, and introduced herself. 'I haven't seen you before,' she finished.

'It's my f-first day on Theatres here,' the nurse revealed and, crying again, continued, 'and probably my l-last.'

Penny went to sit on the desk beside the girl, and put an arm round her shoulders.

'Oh, dear,' she said. 'Have you been in trouble?'

'Yes,' sobbed the nurse. 'It was awful!'

Penny could see that the girl was only about eighteen—a second-year trainee, probably doing her first stint on Theatres. What a ward to send her to! thought Penny.

'What's your name?' she asked, and the girl told her it was Veronica. She was still crying. What on earth could have upset her so much?

'Tell me what happened?' urged Penny gently, and Veronica lifted her tear-stained face from the desk, looking as though she was glad of the command.

'He was doing a craniotomy,' she explained, 'and Scrub-sister had to go into the next theatre for something, and I was left there alone. It's terrible in there. I didn't know what to do. I've n-never been on Th-Theatres before,' she howled.

'He asked me for something,' she continued. 'A-a——I can't even remember, but I found it somehow and gave it to him. I was very s-slow but he didn't s-say anything. But he l-looks so—so. . .'

Penny began to gather they were speaking of Nicholas Adams. 'I think I understand,' she said. 'This would be Dr Adams?'

'Yes,' confirmed Veronica, wiping her face with the back of her hand. 'Well, we went on. I thought I was doing OK. Scrub-sister came back and I felt better. But th-then it happened!' The tears were rolling down again.

Penny waited. 'Mm?' she said.

'I don't know how it happened! He asked me to wipe his forehead. He was holding the—thing—you know——It was a difficult bit, and he was sweating.'

Penny hadn't any idea what 'the thing' could be, but she didn't say so. 'And what happened?' she asked.

'I knocked his hand!' Veronica wailed, crying harder than ever. 'I didn't mean to do it. I don't even know how I did. But I reached across with the sponge, and I knocked his hand.'

Penny stood silent for a moment. 'What did he do?' she asked apprehensively.

'Oh, God!' Veronica groaned, as though the memory appalled her. 'If he'd gone beserk I think I'd have felt better. He looked like he wanted to. But all he did was—s-say things. He told me to get out of the theatre, out of his sight, before he killed me. He spoke to the scrub more than me, asking her how the hell they were supposed to operate with untrained and—and—incompetent idiots——'

Veronica couldn't go on.

'Oh, dear, oh, dear,' groaned Penny, feeling equally sorry for Adams and the girl.

'I can n-never go back in there!' she wailed. 'I'm no good. I'll have to give up nursing!'

'Rubbish,' said Penny firmly, and settled down to try and talk Veronica out of her distress.

It was a difficult task, and at the end of it she seemed no further advanced. Veronica obviously loved nursing, but she was appalled at her mistake, and was just as adamant about leaving at the end of an hour.

Penny wondered if anything but a word from Nicholas Adams would talk her out of it. Once the idea had formed, it took root in her brain.

He must have been very angry, and in anger had said some harsh things. But he also must realise that Veronica was a very inexperienced nurse who had been under the incredible strain of being left alone to do a job she was unprepared for. And everyone made mistakes before they learned.

Penny was inclined to think that Adams ought to be told how seriously she was taking it. He probably didn't realise the effects his words had had. She resolved to talk to the scrub-sister, and advised Veronica to go and eat some lunch, or at least take a walk in the sunshine, rather than sit there crying.

It was too late to talk to Jessie this morning. Lunches would already be on their way. So she sat instead in the nurses' common-room and waited for the 'scrub'. She'd been told the operation was almost over.

The sister was sorry for Veronica. But she didn't seem to feel it would help to tell Dr Adams how upset she was.

'He's not too pleased with me, either, Penny,' she asserted. 'I'm not the one to argue her cause.'

'No, I didn't really mean that,' said Penny. 'I just thought he should know how sorry she is.'

The older girl shook her head. 'If you think so, you tell him Pen. Not me.'

Penny thought about it as she walked downstairs to the dining-room. He'd shown he was a fair man. It wasn't right not to tell him. She'd do it herself.

She had not been sitting down long before Larry joined her. 'My God!' he said. 'You should have been in Theatre this morning. Or rather, you shouldn't.'

'I think I know what you're talking about,' she said. 'I've just spent an hour talking to a rather distressed trainee.'

'Have you, indeed?' Larry said. 'Well, I've no doubt she needed it. We could hear old Nick creating in the next theatre. Apparently bumped his arm, after spending hours passing him the wrong instruments!'

'That was hardly her fault!' said Penny. 'She's a second-year trainee!'

'Tell it to Nick!' replied Larry, with a grin that Penny thought was unfeeling.

'I shall do just that,' she told him.

Larry stopped grinning. 'Then you'll be making a big mistake,' he informed her flatly. 'Leave it alone or you'll cop it next.'

'Rubbish,' said Penny. 'He's not so unfair. She's talking of giving up nursing,' she added.

Larry shrugged his shoulders, and Penny was shocked. 'She was totally unprepared for the job they gave her,' she said hotly.

'Oh, sure, and Adams knew that. He didn't yell at her for being slow or not knowing the names of things. But, Penny, even a moron can wipe a forehead without bumping an arm holding an instrument at the most delicate part of an operation!'

'It's a change to hear you defending the boss,' snapped Penny, stung to retort.

'I'm not defending him. I'm warning you. He was livid, and will be for days. Certainly there are mitigating factors for the girl's mistake. It must have been a strain for her. And Adams was hardly sympathetic. He was what he normally is—though you don't seem to believe it.'

'And what's that?' asked Penny tersely.

'Exacting, unsupportive, totally lacking in understanding of human feelings, punitive and harsh!'

Penny glared at him across the table. She was going to prove him wrong. The Adams she knew was fair. He would give the girl a second chance. She voiced her thoughts.

'You're crazy,' said Larry. 'He wouldn't give a damn what happens to her, and he won't have her back.'

'We'll see,' she replied, and angrily dug at her pudding.

After lunch, Penny made herself a cup of tea and tried to get into the mood to tackle the problem of Jessie. She decided to ask her little friend to the office. Nurse Dobson wheeled Jess in in a chair, and Penny gave her a cup of tea. They sat drinking it, and looking out of the wide window at the world below and beyond the ward.

The view seemed to accomplish Penny's task for her. Without introducing the topic, without saying a word or even asking for Jessie's confidences, Penny received them.

'Penny,' she began softly, watching the cars moving along the road to the city. 'Will I ever leave here?'

With all the preparation Penny had done for this moment, she still felt an almost insuperable difficulty in answering, and Jessie herself filled in the pause.

'Oh, I know I shouldn't ask you that. It's a terrible question.' She gave a little smile.

Penny felt a knife twist in her heart. Jessie was thinking of her. And Penny hated herself suddenly for her own cowardice, in the face of this child's courage. It gave her courage of her own.

'You have a right to ask that question, sweetheart,' she said. 'And a right to have it answered truthfully. People don't answer because—because they love you so, and they know the answer will make you very sad.'

Jessie's brown eyes met hers, and Penny wanted to cry at what they held.

'Will I die here?' the child asked, her voice beginning to waver and break.

Penny herself found it hard to speak for the lump in her throat, and the tears were welling in her own eyes. 'You may do, Jessie,' she said, very softly. 'There may not be much more we can do.'

It was the only way to tell her without taking away all hope. She couldn't do that.

Jessie sobbed. 'Will you be with me, Penny?' she

asked in a pitiful voice, her little face held up bravely to stop the tears from falling. 'Will you promise me that?'

'Yes, darling,' promised Penny, and they clung to each other then, crying in earnest and sharing a sorrow too deep for any other experience.

It was hours later when Penny approached the unit director's office. As sad as the interview just over had been for Jessie, Penny could see that she was relieved to have been told. She had known it in her heart in any case, and now it could be talked about and grieved over.

Penny herself felt weighed down. And despite her protests to Larry about Dr Adams' fairness and about his needing to know about Veronica, the closer she got to his door the more misgivings she had. It was going to be very embarrassing. He might think she was blaming him. Penny tried to think of poor Veronica.

Miss Fosdyke was stationed at her desk, and looked rather scandalised when the little nurse counsellor approached and said she wanted to speak to Dr Adams.

'I'll just see,' the older woman said haughtily, and pressed the intercom button. It was answered sharply. 'Sister Anderson, the nurse counsellor, would like to see you, Doctor,' she said doubtfully, and there was a pause.

'Tell her to come in,' the intercom said shortly, and Penny felt her heart start to pound. It's the right thing to do, she reminded herself. That usually helped, but today didn't seem so effective.

Gingerly she let herself in to his office. He was

seated at his desk, surrounded by files, X-rays and Theatre notes. He looked forbidding. And busy. Penny's heartbeat now was rapid as machine-gun fire. She stood in front of his desk with her hands clasped behind her.

'What can I do for you?' Adams asked, and Penny took a breath.

'It's about Veronica Lang,' she began, and saw him frown.

'Who is she?' he asked.

Penny realised he didn't know the nurse's name. 'Nurse Veronica Lang,' she said. 'Second-year trainee, rostered to Theatres for the first time today.'

Penny saw his eyebrows shoot up. 'What do you know about it?' he fired.

Penny began to explain, but he interrupted her.

'Don't stand there like a carpeted schoolgirl,' he snapped. 'Sit down, for God's sake.'

Penny had never known him so brusque. It unnerved her more.

She sat in the chair by the desk, and told him haltingly about the conversation she had had with the girl that morning.

He was silent as she finished, studying her face in a disconcerting way, and evidently thinking. Finally he spoke.

'And you have come to the conclusion that Nurse Lang has been cruelly mistreated.'

Penny would have immediately disclaimed this assessment of her feelings on the subject, but he did not give her time.

'You may be right. I've no doubt that there are others who would be only too willing to say so.'

Penny thought immediately of Larry.

Adams went on, 'But I don't allow other people's opinions of me to influence my decisions. The nurse performed inadequately. I cannot afford incompetence and carelessness in my staff, and I will not tolerate it.'

Penny was stunned. There was no humanity about his speech. He spoke like a machine. She had thought he would tell her that Lang had been hopeless, that he would chide her for interfering, but she was unprepared for this cold and ruthless approach to the matter. Where was his fairness now?

She forced herself to speak. 'I've spoken to the scrub-sister,' she said in a low voice, devoid of the emotion she was feeling. 'She says she has good reports. She's very new and—lacking confidence. She was rattled.' Penny gave him an appealing look. It was not so much a decision in Nurse Lang's favour she was begging, but a more human approach to the discussion.

It seemed to anger Adams. She saw the muscles in his jaw work, and he didn't speak immediately.

'Sister Anderson,' he said finally, and the title dismayed her, 'I don't want rattled nurses. I want efficient ones——'

Penny interrupted him, ignoring the dangerous edge to his voice, making a last ditch-stand to help Veronica. 'She's going to give up nursing.'

'Damn you!' he said suddenly, and Penny saw him now as the theatre that morning had seen him—about to explode. She flinched, but sat still. 'Go and counsel patients,' he continued. 'Don't come counselling me! I neither need nor want your interference, and Nurse Lang will have to make her own decision about her future. Whatever she decides, she is unfit to work in my theatre and I won't have her there. Now for God's sake, go away!'

Penny sat stock-still for a moment. The blood had ebbed from her face, and was now returning. The rage and frustration in his voice had immobilised her, but she knew she must go.

Without looking at him, she got unsteadily to her feet and left the room. In her office, she let her feelings take over, and fell into her chair with her head on the desk. Then, much as Nurse Lang had done, she cried.

CHAPTER FIVE

WHEN Penny went home that evening, she was glad that Carrie was working. She needed time to sort out her thoughts and feelings, and she could only do it alone. Then, all at once, perversely, she felt lonely. She thought of her family, and wanted above all to be with them. She could phone them, of course, as she did each weekend, but they would know from her voice that something was wrong. And she didn't want to worry them. Especially with something like this, which wasn't really important anyway.

No, it's not, she told herself. So what? A minor quarrel with her boss, who quarrelled with lots of people anyway. What was there in his words to upset her so much?

'Damn you,' he had said, and 'don't come counselling me'. Well, what was so terrible about that? He had said worse to poor Nurse Lang.

But Penny had to admit how much his words and his tone had hurt and angered her. Had she really deserved that? She thought about it hard. She didn't think so. Perhaps she'd deserved to be told to keep out of it, but she hadn't earned the scorn and rage he'd heaped on her. Her own rage mounted as she thought about it. Damn *him*! she thought. He was just like the others, only worse. Arrogant, egotistical, and—Larry's word came back to her—unfeeling.

Larry had been right. 'If you get between him and

his work, he'll turn on you.' And, 'Stay out of it, or you'll cop it next.'

She thought about the doctor who was so gentle with the children, the one they loved. He was a sham, she decided. It was a charming veneer, designed to secure their co-operation. He didn't care about anyone.

But even as she thought it, her conscience assailed her. Perhaps she too now was being unfair. He must care about the children. Could Jess be so wrong? And what about those lunches?

But as she posed herself the question, his words returned to her. 'You can't work well without adequate nutrition.' And the angry part of her seized on them as evidence for the prosecution. He hadn't been concerned for her welfare at all, but only that she would continue to work well. He was interested in keeping his machines going. That was all any of them were to him. Larry, Veronica, the nurses, she herself. They were pieces of hospital equipment which must be kept in good working order. They were no more human to him than the scalpel he held in his hand.

Penny sighed. The hurt and the anger would not go away. She wondered for a moment why she cared so much. She had certainly never enjoyed being the focus of people's anger and disapproval, but there was more to it than that. Perhaps her pride was hurt, too. She had been mistaken in him. She had even defended him to Larry. And now he could say 'I told you so'. Was that what hurt so much?

She had thought he was fair. She had even admired him. She turned the thought over. Yes, it was true.

For all his severity, she had admired him. He was a good doctor. She had thought him a good man.

Well, she thought bitterly, it's never too late to learn.

The evening for Nurse Lang was more satisfactory.

She was miserably smoking cigarettes in the common-room when one of the other nurses called her to the phone. Nurse Lang got up listlessly, unable to think of a single person she really wanted to talk to, unless it was perhaps that nice nurse counsellor. Nurse Lang picked up the receiver.

It seemed that she wasn't called upon to contribute much to the conversation going on. Nor, in truth, could she have done so. The circumstance of being telephoned by the director of the unit was enough to deprive her of all powers of speech.

Little that she said, however, Nurse Lang's conversation seemed to have a powerful effect on her. She replaced the receiver shakily, and walked automatically back to the common-room, an enormous smile of relief spreading over her features and tears of gratitude springing to her eyes.

Her friend had come in from the wards. 'What's this I hear, Ronnie?' asked the blonde young trainee with concern. 'Walters said you were leaving!'

Veronica smiled at her. 'I don't think I will, after all' she replied.

When Penny arrived at work that morning, she found Larry waiting for her in her office. She was not very pleased. She never locked the door, but that didn't mean that people could walk in as they chose. She was equally displeased with his greeting.

'Good morning, sweetheart,' he said, and made a move as if to embrace her.

'I'm not your sweetheart,' she answered firmly, and sat down behind her desk.

'Oh, dear,' Larry smiled ruefully. 'Still mad at me, are you? Really, Penny, I'm sorry if I upset you, but you've got to face the truth. Adams is not the hero you think he is.'

Since this statement echoed Penny's own thoughts on the subject, it was unaccountable, she felt, that it should make her angry. But it did.

'Larry, I really don't want to talk about him,' she said, controlling herself.

'Good,' he replied. 'Let's talk about us, then.'

'I don't want to talk about that, either,' she snapped.

She really felt rather raw this morning. 'I'm sorry, Larry,' she tendered. 'I'm not in a very good mood.'

'I see that,' he replied, cheerfully enough. 'Perhaps it will improve as the day goes on.' With that he departed, and Penny was left to hope this didn't mean that he was coming back. She had seen quite enough of Larry Stevenson in the last few days to last her a good few weeks.

Penny went, with a rather heavy heart, to visit Jessica. She was glad she had gone. Jessie had been waiting anxiously to see her. Having absorbed yesterday's news and had a little time to think about it, she wanted to discuss it further.

'How long will I live?' she asked Penny directly, and Penny was nonplussed. She had heard the doctors' estimates—about three to six months, they thought.

But it seemed such a terrible sentence, and she really didn't know what the inside and outside limits were. It was not fair to Jessie to give that estimate without knowing the possibilities.

Penny frowned. 'I'm not sure, Jessie,' she admitted.

'A year?' the child asked hopefully.

'Maybe,' Penny replied, and made a decision. 'I'll have to ask Dr Nicholas. You know that no one can be sure. To some extent it depends on you.'

Penny wondered if the twelve-year-old girl would understand, and was relieved when she seemed to.

Jessie nodded. 'I know,' she said. 'But you see, I have to get an idea. There are things I want to do.'

Penny smiled at her. How like her to take it like this. She was braver even than little Meg had been. Penny was glad that she had told her. How awful if death had approached Jess unawares, and she hadn't done those things.

Penny promised to see Dr Adams that day. Inwardly, she groaned. It was the very last thing she wanted to do. But there was no choice. They had to work together.

She combed Jessie's hair for her now, in preparation for her parents' visit. Jessie seemed worried about it.

'Will my parents know I know?' she asked Penny.

'If you like, I'll tell them,' Penny offered.

The child thought a while. 'No,' she said at last. 'I'd better, Penny.'

Penny nodded, knowing what she meant. It would be a relief for there to be no more secrets between them, for the family to be able to grieve together.

Penny arranged for Jessie to see her parents in the Quiet Room, and then came back to tell her about a new little girl, brought in with the same sort of symptoms that Jessica had had.

Jessie was genuinely sad. 'Why does it have to happen?' she asked.

Penny shook her head. 'I don't know, Jess. For some reason hidden from us, God wants it to be.'

Jessie accepted the statement with a tremulous smile. 'Will she die, too?' she asked.

'Maybe not,' Penny answered. 'We don't know yet.'

'I hope not,' said Jess. 'I think it must be nice to live to be sixteen, and be able to wear make-up and go out with boys, and stuff.' Her little voice was sad.

Penny had an idea. 'Lots of girls wear make-up before they're sixteen,' she remarked, and looked at Jessie questioningly.

Jessie caught her meaning, and sat up in bed.

'Oh, Penny,' she cried excitedly. 'Do you think I could?' The hopefulness in her tone caught at Penny's heart. It was such a little thing.

'I'm sure we could persuade your mother to let you,' Penny replied. 'I'm certainly going to try.'

'Thank you, Penny. It's such a wonderful idea.'

Penny said goodbye before she could burst into tears in the ward.

She cried, instead, in her office, asking Jessie's question. Why did it have to be this way? And why Jessie? She thought, too, about Jessie's other question. She would have to speak to Dr Adams today. He was the only one who could answer her, and it wasn't fair to keep her waiting.

And her heart thumped suddenly at a new thought. She hadn't consulted him before telling Jessie as much as she had.

Perhaps she ought have. She thought of their discussion on the very first day. 'You may be right in some cases', he had said. Would he feel that this was one of those cases? Would he feel she ought have asked him anyway? Penny had a sinking feeling that the answer to the last question might well be yes. Damn. She'd really done nothing but get into scrapes since she'd got here. So much for a low profile.

But her anger came to her aid. Too bad, she told herself. I've done the right thing. I know it. That's all that matters. He told me I was on my own, and he's made no attempt to guide me. And if he treats his staff the way he treated me yesterday, he can't be surprised when they don't consult him.

Thus fortified, she found herself equal to the task of writing a note asking him for a brief few minutes that day. She took it along to Miss Fosdyke before she could lose her nerve.

Late in the afternoon her note was answered, not by a call from Miss Fosdyke to say come along to Dr Adams' office, as she had expected, but by a knock on her own door and the presence of Dr Adams himself.

The unexpectedness of it flustered her for a moment, but the sight of him brought back his words of yesterday, and rekindled her anger. It steadied her.

'I received your note,' he said.

Penny found she did not want to meet his eyes.

'Thank you for coming,' she said stiffly. 'There was no need, though. You could have sent for me. Would you care to sit down?'

There was silence for a moment, and Penny was forced to look up at him. She wished at once that she hadn't. His eyes looked intently into hers from a distance of three feet, and her heart gave that same nervous lurch she had experienced on their first meeting.

The muscles in her jaw tightened. Something had happened to Penny since yesterday. She had made a decision. She was not going to let him intimidate her any more. With a polite gesture, she indicated a chair.

'Thank you,' he said at last, and took it.

'I wanted to speak with you about Jess, as I said in my note.' Penny took a slow breath. 'She wants to know how long she has.'

He answered slowly. 'She knows she is dying?' he said. It was a question.

'Yes, she does. I discussed it with her.' Penny knew the tone of her voice was defiant. She didn't care. She was prepared for attack, and determined to defend herself.

He let out a long breath. And then his words surprised her. 'That can't have been easy. I'm grateful to be spared that task, but it must have been painful for you.'

The gentle sympathy in his voice took her by surprise. It was as different from yesterday's tone as it could possibly be. And in an instant, Penny was aware of another danger. As little as she meant to be intimidated by Nicholas Adams, nor did she wish to show him her feelings about Jess. She would always have been loath to let her boss see how her work could affect her, but with Adams it was doubly important. She mustn't show him any weakness. In the first place, her pride demanded it. And in the second, she didn't trust him. Perhaps he would feel she was too emotional for the job—weak, immature, unsuitable.

But his caring tone had already accomplished what no abuse or blame this morning could have done. She had felt her defences shake and crumble, and all her pain at Jess's tragedy well up in her. Her throat grew tight and the tears pricked at her eyes.

She felt her command begin to slip from her, and a kind of panic seized her. She *must* not cry in front of this man.

Abruptly she turned away, just as Nicholas Adams made a small movement as though to get up.

'It's all right,' she said quickly. 'That's my job.'

It had taken some control to keep her voice steady. But she had managed it, even if it had sounded harsh; and she managed to go on. 'I know you've said three months. But I need to know the limits.'

'Yes,' she heard him say. 'That is my guess. But it's only a guess. It's never really possible to say. And it's important not to take away all hope. I—don't have to tell you that, I know.' He sighed. 'I would say. . .three months to one year are the limits.'

Penny turned from the window. 'Thank you,' she said steadily. She forced herself to meet his eyes again and to keep her face impassive, but it was difficult. For his face held an expression she had only seen before when he had bent down to comfort one of his patients. It was caring, compassionate, even tender.

It was a sham, she told herself angrily, and she stared hard at the papers on her desk.

'Well,' she said. 'That was all I wanted to know Dr Adams. I know you're very busy. I won't take up more of your time.'

Nicholas Adams might have been about to speak,

but at this point he changed his mind. Wearily, it seemed, he got up to leave.

Penny felt a sense of triumph. She had mastered the feelings which had threatened to overwhelm her. She hadn't let him see how upset she was. She hadn't broken down. And, even better, she hadn't blushed and hadn't stammered in his presence. She had been businesslike and to the point. Perhaps she had also been brusque, and close to rude. She was aware that her last statement had been perilously close to a dismissal of him, and not what was expected of a junior staff member. But she didn't care. Penny couldn't feel that she owed him any extraordinary civility after his treatment of her yesterday. All in all, it served him right if she had been rude.

Now she had to see Jess again. She had her answer. A year at most, unless there was a miracle. And miracles, reflected Penny grimly, seemed rather thin on the ground these days.

It was another painful interview. She explained to Jess that there was always hope, that they would keep trying to help her. But she knew how faint that slim hope was. And she could see that Jess knew it too, perhaps had known it long since.

At the end of it, Penny felt numb and battered. The day had seemed endless. Perhaps it had been the same for some of the other staff on children's neuro. As Penny passed the nurses' desk there seemed to be a full-scale battle going on.

Penny thought about the cheerful camaraderie of the nursing staff at the last place she had worked, and felt sad for them all.

When she again reached her office, she once again found Larry installed there.

'Did the day improve, my sweet?' he asked her.

Wearily, Penny sat down. 'No,' she said without thinking, 'and it's not looking up now.'

Larry said nothing, and Penny saw that she had wounded him. She was sorry. It had been nothing more than a thoughtless jest. No, that was not right. It had been nothing less than the truth. But she was not in the habit of dealing out such truths. She was contrite.

'I'm sorry, Larry,' she said. 'It has been a difficult day. I didn't mean to say that.' That, at least, was true.

He looked slightly mollified. 'You can soothe my wounded feelings by making me a cup of tea,' he suggested and Penny complied, though she longed to go home.

'Now, let me see you smile,' he urged, and she did so grudgingly. 'Not very good,' he observed. 'I know, I'll tell you a joke I heard on men's medical.'

He told her the joke, and dutifully she laughed, to heal the breach. If only he would go! She wished him at the devil.

It might have been a sentiment shared by Nicholas Adams at that moment. He had waited till Penny had finished with Jessica to make her a second visit. Now he was prevented by the presence of Larry Stevenson in her office. The sound of laughter drifted through the half-open door.

Nicholas gave it up. He turned and strode off down the corridor.

CHAPTER SIX

PENNY was glad for the coming of the weekend. She knew she would feel much happier after two days away from the ward, and she arranged to have all her time taken up in pursuits so different from her daily ones that she wouldn't even think of the hospital. On Sunday she borrowed a little sailing boat from a friend, and she and Carrie went for a sail on the harbour.

It was a lovely day, if exhausting. The sun shone brilliantly and a gentle spring breeze was blowing, as the two girls tacked down the blue waterway, avoiding ferries, tugs and other pleasure craft with more luck than expertise.

They dropped the anchor in a sheltered cove at lunchtime, and sat in the sun, contentedly eating the food they had brought, and talking. The conversation inevitably turned to work in general, and Dr Adams in particular, for now Carrie was in possession of the facts of the last few days. But Penny did not mind. Sitting here on their gently rocking little craft in the sun, she felt remote enough from the subject of discussion to be untroubled by it.

Carrie, a nurse herself, had been very sympathetic to poor Nurse Lang when Penny had told her about it. Now she returned to the discussion.

'It's quite incredible,' she was saying 'that a nurse that junior should be left in that situation.'

Penny agreed.

'You know, with that sort of nursing staff shortage, it's amazing they hired a nurse counsellor for the team. I'd have thought they'd want another general nurse.'

'There's an awful lot of work in the unit that really is counselling work,' Penny replied. 'But, yes. I know what you mean. Perhaps that's why I'm so unpopular with Sister Berensen.'

Penny mused on the idea a moment, and concluded that it would explain a lot of Berensen's behaviour.

'I wonder if Adams wanted a nurse counsellor?' Carrie said.

Penny thought back to the beginning when Dr Adams had missed her interview, and to their first meeting, when he had sounded so bitter about the shortage of nursing and medical staff.

She felt surprised that she had not thought of it before.

'No,' she said. 'No, now that I think of it, he almost certainly didn't.' She gave a short, mirthless laugh. 'I should have realised that. We've probably been destined to be enemies from the start.'

Carrie looked at her. 'It seems funny to hear *you* talking about enemies, Pen. You've probably never had one in your life.'

'Well, I do now,' she replied with a rueful grin.

'I've never seen you angry like this. Not even when someone was unfair to you. You always made excuses for them.'

Penny was silent awhile. 'Mm,' she said at last. 'Only I just can't think of any excuses good enough this time.'

'He was very tired,' Carrie suggested.

'Everyone's very tired, Carrie. It's—it's not enough

to be a brilliant surgeon. If you're going to lead a unit like that, you need some—compassion for those you work with. Some feelings. Real feelings, I mean. He can—he can seem as though he cares. I've seen him do it. But it's all bedside manner. As Larry says, he can be very charming. But there's nothing underneath it. It's all pretence.'

'I know what you mean, Pen. Some of them don't have any real feelings left. I think they all had them once. They just get—sort of—crushed out of them.'

Penny nodded. And she suddenly felt very sad. It seemed suddenly such a tragic waste that he should be like that.

'I don't think you'd better fall for him after all, old girl,' she heard Carrie say. 'I think you'd better go for Larry Stevenson.'

Penny looked at her incredulously, then realised her friend was joking.

'Nuts to that!' she cried, laughing. 'I won't go for any of them.'

Penny returned to the ward refreshed and suntanned on Monday morning. It was as well she was refreshed. The unit was working at the usual frantic pace, with several accident victims having been brought in over the weekend. One child had been flown by helicopter from the country after he had fallen under a tractor. It was a nasty case which would require major surgery.

Adams was there with him in the part of the ward kept for acute cases, and there were other doctors too. The boy was a mass of tubes, as far as Penny could see, and a respirator was breathing for him.

She was wondering whether this was one of the

patients who might be thought better off if he did not survive, when Adams called her over.

Gingerly she approached the bed, braving Berensen's hostile glance, and awaited Dr Adams' instructions.

He seemed absorbed in his task. He flicked his eyes up at Penny and back again to the boy, and spoke as he worked. It was in the manner of a senior doctor lecturing his interns, the tone calm and measured.

'This eight-year-old boy has suffered a fractured skull and subdural haematoma as a result of an accident. He needs——' he broke off a moment to concentrate frowningly on what he was doing '—extensive surgery this morning. As well as his head injury, he has a flail chest and a collapsed lung, and probably a damaged spleen. These all need attention as soon as possible. Dr Knight——' he named one of the eminent general surgeons '—is coming to see him as well.'

Penny waited, as he straightened up to draw up an injection.

'His parents are here,' the doctor told her. 'They need some help. I've had little time to talk with them and, in any case, at this stage it's impossible to say whether the child will pull through.'

Penny wondered at the matter-of-factness of his tone. She knew at that moment that she had chosen her career well. She could never have been a surgeon. To be able to regard the pale little person lying in this bed as a collection of organs, which might be made to function again, or might not, was utterly impossible for her.

With a muttered, 'I'll see them,' she left the team to their unenviable task, and went to find the parents.

It was easy to see why Adams had told her to attend to them. They were in an awful state, their nightmare made worse by the fact of having had no sleep during the night. Arranging quarters for them where they might collapse in exhaustion for a few hours seemed to Penny a high priority.

With so many critical cases in, the atmosphere on the ward that day was as strained as it had been on Friday. It seemed to filter through to the patients, who in response became abnormally difficult.

The nurses were short-handed and short-tempered, and Penny could cheerfully have flung something at a number of them, whose brusqueness had upset their small patients.

They seemed to have no idea of how to support one another under the strain, and snapped and bickered instead. Penny began to think that it was not so much a team of nurses who worked here but a collection of isolated individuals, battling along alone under intolerable burdens.

Why didn't Nicholas Adams do something about the morale on his unit? she thought impatiently. And then gave an inward laugh at herself. What did he care about that? Machines didn't need morale. Adams was probably the very reason that morale *was* so low.

Penny found herself angrier with him than ever. He was a fool, she decided. If the unit got along better, it would work better. Couldn't he see how bad things were? Hadn't he ever spent five minutes thinking what could be done about it?

She wondered what, if anything, *could* be done about it. It was stressful work. There was too much of it. There were too few workers, and poor communication between them. Their failures were heart-breaking, and sometimes the 'successes' scarcely less so.

Penny wondered suddenly whether anyone here ever discussed these things. Did they ever talk together about their difficulties? Their fears? The heartache? Did they ever share the pain of nursing children who often died?

The germ of an idea was sprouting in Penny's mind. Why shouldn't there be a time put aside for talking about these things? Why not have, say, a fortnightly meeting especially for that purpose? It could be at lunchtime. They could all eat together. It would have to be all of them, though. How could she arrange an hour together for the entire nursing staff of children's neuro once a fortnight?

It seemed a difficult prospect. Nicholas Adams was the logical person to consult about it, but Penny shrank from that. Doubtless he would see it as an attempt on her part to counsel the staff. He wouldn't see the necessity for it. It would be interference, a waste of precious time. The unit was so busy now. How could they all leave the ward for an hour? There was no way Adams would be sympathetic to the idea.

Perhaps Penny would have forgotten the idea but for the rancorous exchange she witnessed not an hour later between two senior nurses she both liked and respected.

It was over a trivial matter—a piece of equipment not restored to its usual place on the shelves. It wasn't far away. It took only a few seconds to find it. Under normal conditions, it was a circumstance not worthy of mention.

But these were not normal conditions. And the argument that ensued over its cost not only time, but a great deal more in human terms.

For struggles like these formed the basis for hurts and enmities which grew as time went on to further poison the life of the ward.

And it had nothing to do with where the nebuliser was put—Penny was certain of that. The real issues were never mentioned. Nurse Donaldson's patient, seeming to rally yesterday and justify all her hopeful care, today was clearly slipping away while the nurse looked on in bitter helplessness.

Penny felt a hard knot of anger and hurt for them in her stomach. Why did it have to be this way? They should be supporting each other. They should be talking about it. They should be sharing it.

Had Carrie been there, she would have recognised the expression on Penny's face now. It was the one which had surprised others—a look of passionate determination.

Damn Adams! Something had to be done about it. These were caring, dedicated people. They deserved better.

And a sudden inspiration made her think of the director of social work. She would be interested. Penny was certain she'd help. She would discuss it with her. And meanwhile she would do what she could to help with the work.

Penny looked about for things she could usefully do for them. One of the things that was sometimes neglected when they were busy was the giving of pain relief. Regular medications that were given, say, four-hourly, were attended to by Sister Berensen. These had to be given on the dot and signed for. Pain relief, however, was usually ordered 'as necessary', so that the timing of doses was left to the nurses' discretion. That meant that either the patient had to make it known that he needed a tablet or injection, or some-one had to discover that it was needed.

Tentatively, Penny approached Sister Berensen to offer to supervise the giving of pain relief. She was a little surprised to find that Berensen agreed with alacrity. Apparently even she was feeling the strain.

'All narcotics have to be accounted for,' the sister warned. 'Write what you give and to whom in the book, and don't get it wrong, or someone will think you're swiping narcotics.'

Penny was familiar with the system most hospitals use to guard against illicit use of narcotic drugs by their employees. She promised to be careful, and began by taking some morphine out of the locked cabinet for the little boy in the bed next to Timmy's.

Penny glowed with satisfaction whenever she saw Timmy now. His health had improved as markedly as his appetite when it had been finally established in a meeting with his parents that his mother was no longer intending to leave them when he came home. The stress of money troubles and a sick child had put alarming strain on Timmy's parents' marriage, but Mrs Holt had never really meant those words which Timmy had overheard. They would battle on together.

Penny was pleased to see it. They were a nice family.

Penny made the time to go to the social-work

meeting that week. She wanted to discuss her idea for the nurses' meetings with Mrs Durham.

'I think it's a wonderful idea!' Mrs Durham exclaimed. 'Someone should have thought of it before.'

'The problem is,' said Penny, 'that everyone would need to be there for it to work. And that would leave the ward with no one.'

Mrs Durham looked thoughtful. 'Perhaps we can solve that problem. It's only for an hour. Why can't we arrange some nursing cover from somewhere else in the hospital? Maybe a ward which would like to run a reciprocal scheme. They could cover for children's neuro for an hour, and neuro could cover for them. I think the Casualty staff might do it. They've been trying to find time to have some special training meetings.'

Penny felt excited. It was possible.

'I haven't discussed it with Dr Adams yet,' she confessed. 'I haven't even discussed it with the nurses.'

'Let me talk to the casualty supervisor first,' said Enid Durham. 'We'll see if it's a possibility.'

Work here was not always enjoyable, Penny reflected as she left the hospital that Friday evening, but it was rewarding. The children were wonderful, and she was making some firm friends among the nursing staff.

The only problems were Berensen and Adams, and even Berensen had been more pleasant lately. Adams she was avoiding as much as she could. When their work brought them together, she was coolly civil, and escaped from him as soon as possible. She felt she was coping very well.

He, for his part, was as polite as he had been on the first day. He didn't rail at her again, or show any anger. Nor did he apologise. Perhaps he just expected her to forgive him automatically, thought Penny bitterly. And then she smiled at herself. More likely he couldn't care less.

There was only one occasion on which she thought his anger was about to resurface.

He had come by as she was doing a dressing.

'Do we force you to do ordinary nursing tasks as well, Sister Anderson?' he'd asked. 'No wonder your days are long.' He had lowered himself on to the bed beside her.

'I'm very happy to help, Dr Adams,' she'd replied, shortly.

She had reached for the tape and was endeavouring to tear a piece off with her teeth while holding the dressing in place with her other hand.

Perhaps it had been his very proximity to her as he'd leant over and offered to help that had provoked the sharpness of her reply.

'There's really no need, Dr Adams,' she said, and realised as she said it that she had positively snapped at him.

He didn't move immediately, but sat facing her with an expression that told of the emotion her rudeness had awakened in him. She saw his eyes fill with it, and a flush creep over his neck.

She held her breath, wondering if he would tear up at her here in front of their patient.

But then he sat back, and Penny thought for a moment that he looked more sad than angry. Without a further word, he got up and left.

It was easier after that, for she no longer seemed to see much of him at all.

And then came the incident that seemed to turn things upside-down for her again. It had been two full weeks since any of the theatre cases had needed her to go with them. But this morning there was one little girl who was decidedly reluctant to leave the ward. She would have to go up there.

They were running late, as usual. Frantic nurses seemed to be running to and fro, muttering under their breaths. One of them, wheeling a machine into Theatre number one, looked familiar.

Penny realised with a shock that it was Veronica Lang.

The shock was fast followed by a glow of relief and pleasure. So she hadn't given up nursing. And she'd even come back to Theatres for another try. Brave girl! Perhaps a good night's sleep had made all the difference.

She must be working with one of the other surgeons, thought Penny, remembering Adams' words.

But, when Penny walked into number one beside her little patient, she found this supposition entirely wrong, and the scene that met her eyes astonished her.

Around the table, the team was ready. Nurse Lang was scrubbed, and standing beside the theatre sister. And Nicholas Adams stood on the other side of the table.

Penny stared. For a moment, she couldn't concentrate on her small charge. Her eyes went from Veronica to the surgeon and met his grey ones for just an instant before he looked down at his feet. Penny waited for him to look up again. She wanted more than anything in the world to put her feelings into a smile. But he seemed to be studying his surgical overshoes with close attention.

She had to attend to her patient.

Out in the corridor afterwards, she did smile. One of the other sisters saw her.

'We don't smile round here, you know,' she said jokingly, and Penny laughed aloud.

'I was glad to see Nurse Lang here,' commented Penny.

The other woman nodded. 'Yes. Amazing,' she said. 'You know what happened don't you? About her coming back?'

Penny shook her head uncertainly.

The sister pulled her aside into the medication-room. 'I shouldn't be spreading this. Ronnie told me and she said she wasn't supposed to. But it's all right to tell you. He rang her up!'

Penny stared at her.

The sister nodded. 'Adams. He rang her up and apologised! Told her to come back the next day. Something, eh?'

Penny swallowed hard. Yeah. Something, she thought. Somehow, she stumbled a reply. It didn't matter. The sister had expected her to be amazed.

But amazed was not quite the word for what she felt, Penny reflected, as she headed for her office. Rotten was the only word that came to mind. She sat in her chair and bit her lip, her head in her hands. He had not only allowed her back. He had invited her back. And apologised.

Penny groaned aloud. Why hadn't somebody told

her? She could have thanked him, or—or at least been civilised and friendly instead of. . .

Penny rapidly reviewed her behaviour towards Nicholas Adams over the past few weeks. The inescapable fact was that she had lost no opportunity afforded her to show him a cold formality which was frankly insolent and offensive.

There was no denying it. He had repented of his harshness the very next day. He had made amends. She had continued to punish him ever since.

Perhaps he didn't care, thought Penny, but was unable to sustain this comfortable fiction as she recalled refusing his help with the dressing.

No. He had cared. It had upset him. She had seen the flush steal up his neck, and had seen his face freeze. She had been extremely successful in antagonising him, she thought.

And all unjustly. It made her groan anew.

But then a small stubborn voice arose in her defence.

Wait just a minute, it announced. He may have relented. He may have done a very decent thing there. But he was damnably rude and unpleasant in the first place. Does subsequent action wipe that out?

Justice having stuck its foot in the door, however, it now seemed determined to have its full say.

He was undoubtedly very rude, it argued. He was almost more tired than you have ever been, and under more stress. Think what it must have cost him to apologise to a junior nurse. Not just to tell her she should come back and try again, but to own himself wrong, unjust.

And if he seems unfeeling sometimes, can you blame

him? Think what he has to do. Remember that injured child with all the tubes? Remember how glad you were that it was his job to try and make that little body work again, not yours? How could he function if he let himself feel it all?

But he said such cruel things! the other voice cried.

Penny shook her head to still the debate that was raging inside it. One thing only was clear. Where Nicholas Adams was concerned, one had better learn to expect the unexpected.

'Will the real Nicholas Adams please stand up?' said Penny exasperatedly.

CHAPTER SEVEN

'So YOU see,' Penny said to Carrie, 'I've been really awful to him, and m-maybe he doesn't deserve it.'

Carrie covered her eyes with her hand. 'Oh, Penelope,' she sighed.

'I know,' said Penny miserably.

'If only someone had told you!' cried Carrie.

They fell silent for a space.

'What do you think of him now?' asked Carrie at length.

Penny shook her head. 'I just don't know any more. He's a complete riddle. I do know one thing. That low profile I was going to keep—you're about to see it.'

Carrie laughed.

But it was not so easy when Penny went back to work on Monday to carry out that plan. For a start, her ideas for a lunchtime supportive meeting seemed to be coming to fruition. Mrs Durham rang her up on Monday morning to say she had spoken to the casualty charge sister, and they thought it was an excellent idea. It would give them an hour for a lecture. They'd be happy to do it once a week if the girls from neuro wanted.

That meant seeing Nicholas Adams. The very thought of it made Penny want to dig a hole and crawl into it. And yet she also wanted to try and undo some of the damage. She wondered if she dared comment on Veronica's presence in Theatre. It might be the last

TAKE FOUR
BEST SELLER ROMANCES
FREE!

♥

Best Sellers are for the true romantic! These stories are our favourite Romance titles re-published by popular demand.

♥

And to introduce to you this superb series, we'll send you four Best Sellers absolutely FREE when you complete and return this card.

♥

We're so confident that you will enjoy Best Sellers that we'll also reserve a subscription for you to the Mills & Boon Reader Service, which means you could enjoy...

Four new novels
sent direct to you every two months (before they're available in the shops).

Free postage and packing
we pay all the extras.

Free regular Newsletter
packed with special offers, competitions, author news and much, much more.

CLAIM YOUR FREE GIFTS OVERLEAF

thing he wanted. He had avoided her eye when he'd seen her there. Perhaps it would make him angry again. Penny realised that she really didn't want to see that.

She went to see him after the morning's Theatre. Surprisingly, Miss Fosdyke put up little fight for once, and pressed the intercom switch directly. I'm wearing her down, thought Penny. It cheered her for the task ahead.

Nicholas Adams was eating some lunch. He was in his rolled up shirt-sleeves, and hadn't put his tie back on after Theatre. She'd never seen him like that. He had strong arms, and a surgeon's sinewy, well-shaped hands. He screwed up his lunch-paper and tossed it with unerring aim into the waste-paper basket as Penny came forward.

She had carefully prepared her speech. She had even practised it last night, but it had been much easier without those disconcerting eyes on her.

She took a deep breath, and first spoke quickly and a little confusedly; then, as he sat immobile and attentive, she warmed to her topic and spoke more confidently and with conviction.

'You see,' she finished. 'I think it may do quite a lot for morale. Of course, I haven't spoken to the nurses about it yet. You might not like the idea.'

Nicholas Adams didn't answer at once. He seemed to be subjecting her face to a lengthy scrutiny. It was hard to read what was in his own. Did he interpret her idea as a criticism? She had tried not to make it sound that way.

'I like the idea,' he said at length.

Penny realised she'd been holding her breath, for it rushed out now in an audible sigh of relief. She smiled.

And now that slow half-smile she had seen before curved Adams' lips in reply, and she thought all at once how beautifully shaped his mouth was, and how it softened the strong lines of his face. And for some reason the reflection seemed to make her heart hammer and to cause a curious tightness in her chest.

'We'll have to make sure the unit is adequately manned,' he was musing. 'I can discuss that further with the casualty officer. You'd better talk to the nursing staff.'

Penny nodded. It was all she could manage just then.

He sat back in his chair and surveyed her again. 'I must thank you, Penny, for thinking of several ideas that ought have been thought of years ago.'

The unexpected accolade made her blush furiously, a reaction not diminished by his keeping his eyes on her. She mumbled something in reply, and began to think about escaping the room.

But he had something more to say to her. His voice when he said it was low. 'Penny, am I always so intimidating?'

And his eyes on her now seemed to stop her from breathing altogether. Nor could she reply.

'Or just—unlikeable?' he finished, so softly that she couldn't be sure she had heard it right.

Penny swallowed twice, and groped in her mind for an answer. 'I—no. It's—I have a problem with authority,' she blurted.

His eyes did not move. 'That's how you see me,' he said tonelessly.

Penny realised it was a question. She had no idea how to answer it.

'Not—not entirely, of course,' she began, then stopped to moisten her lips. Her face was aflame, her whole body abominably hot. 'I—you——'

She realised suddenly that her ears were ringing, and that she felt light-headed. She shook her head to stop it, and the room seemed to tilt and spin. She clutched the arms of her chair to steady herself and closed her eyes.

His voice seemed to come from a long way off, though she knew he must be close because he was touching her.

'Slowly,' he was saying. 'Breathe slowly. More slowly still. Good girl.'

One of his hands was on her wrist, the other had pressed her head down on to her knees and was stroking the back of her head with slow, rhythmic strokes. It felt good. It was gentle, comforting. She matched her breathing to its rhythm, and slowly the tingling in her fingers stopped, and the buzzing in her head receded.

She became aware that he was kneeling beside her. She turned her head and her eyes focused on his hand, its strong fingers resting on her wrist, one on her radial pulse.

She let out a long breath. 'I felt dizzy,' she explained.

'You breathed too fast,' he answered. 'Hyperventilated.' His other hand stopped its stroking and rested gently on her hair. 'It was my fault,' he said quietly. 'I'm sorry. I shouldn't have asked you such an impossible question.'

Penny took another long breath, and sat back in her chair.

'I'm such a coward,' she said.

Nicholas Adams stayed where he was a moment, looking at her, then said in a low voice, 'Not you. . . You're all right, now,' he added, getting up. 'Just sit there for five minutes.'

Penny nodded obediently.

'I should get a chance to speak to the casualty director today,' he went on. 'There's no reason why you shouldn't get started with your meetings in the next week or so.'

Penny realised he was talking to put her at her ease. She was grateful. But she knew that she could only relax when she was alone, and when, finally, he consented to her getting up and going, her relief was heartfelt.

Back in her own room, she lay back in her chair, feeling as puzzled as she was embarrassed.

Why had he asked her that? Did her diffidence annoy him? When she had put it aside and been assertive, that had annoyed him more. He had been right. It was an impossible question. Penny thought of what she might have said in answer if the absolute truth could have been told.

Intimidating? Yes, you are. You're powerful and you shout at people and say cutting things when they displease you. You're exacting and impatient, and you have an oddly penetrating gaze which is the most intimidating thing of all. Also, you're too attractive. That somehow makes it worse, though I don't know why it should. All in all, Dr Adams, you intimidate me so much I can hardly breathe in your presence, and my heart hammers.

But it's not all your fault. I've always been easily intimidated. It's something to do with my upbringing.

And the thought of making such a speech to Nicholas Adams, and the effect it would have on him, suddenly awakened Penny's sense of humour. She couldn't help herself. She laughed out loud.

Another thought occurred to her. She knew suddenly why the children trusted him, how it was that his touch could calm them so effectively. There was something wonderfully comforting about his presence when something was wrong. His hands were gentle and yet sure. She remembered the sensation of his hand on her wrist, and his touch on her head. It had felt so good—so—so safe, she thought. It hadn't mattered that days before he had shouted at her. His caressing hand had stroked it all away.

Penny sighed as she reviewed the stormiest work relationship she had ever had. One thing was certain. As kind as Dr Adams had been, it wasn't going to make it any easier to deal with him. With the embarrassment of this episode to remember, she was likely to feel more awkward with him that ever.

'What gets to me is that it's always the nicest kids who seem to die,' said Jeanna Wallace, and the others agreed.

They were sitting in the room where the ward meetings were held, but the atmosphere was far different than it was on those occasions.

It had started out much the same. The nurses were stiff with each other at first, and uncertain as to what they were meant to do. They had agreed readily enough to eating their lunches together today while casualty nurses filled in for them. Even Sister Berensen, though inclined to be sarcastic, had agreed when she'd learned that Nicholas Adams thought a fortnightly nurses' meeting a good idea.

Penny explained that the purpose of the meeting would be to discuss whatever they wanted. It could be roster changes or ward work routines or problems with patients.

And because she knew it would be difficult to start, she began with some thoughts of her own.

She had been thinking what a shame it was that Jess would have to spend what time she had left in hospital. If her parents had lived in the city here, perhaps she might have gone home for a while.

It was a good place to start. Few could help but love Jess.

And soon discussion was in full swing, on this and many other problems of work on the unit.

When, in the final minutes, Penny looked around, she could see how much the feeling in the group had changed. They were relaxed now. They were leaning back in their chairs. Some had kicked their shoes off. They were talking to one another in a way that many of them had never done before.

It was a roaring success.

Nicholas Adams sought her on the ward later, and asked her how it had gone.

'It went well,' she said.

'Good,' he told her. He sounded sincere. He looked at her a moment. 'How are you?' he asked.

Penny blushed. 'I'm fine,' she said, and swallowed. 'I don't normally do things like that. I'm sorry.'

There was a short silence. 'There's nothing for you

to be sorry about,' he assured her, and added, almost to himself, 'but rather a lot for me.'

Penny pondered on it later. It was probably as close as he would ever get to an apology over Veronica Lang. She was grateful that he hadn't said more. She would have given a lot to have developed total amnesia for the whole affair.

Several days later Jessie's mother arrived at the ward with a number of interesting-looking packages.

It was make-up. And Jessie was thrilled at the surprise.

Mrs Brand couldn't stay long, so it was Penny who remained with Jessica to try it out. They sat together in one corner of the day-room, exclaiming over the bottles and jars and lipsticks Mrs Brand had bought, and giggling together like a couple of teenagers.

Penny felt every bit as excited as Jessica was, and it was a long time before they were able to decide what colours in eyeshadow, lipstick and blusher to use.

Penny began to make Jess up in order to show her how, while Jess watched every move Penny made in the mirror she held. The process was accompanied by chattering and giggling from them both, and so much from Jessica that it seemed it would be impossible for Penny to apply the lipstick.

'Hold still,' she laughed, 'or you're going to have lipstick from one ear to the other!'

'Oh, I'm so excited, I can't!' cried Jess. 'Do you think Dr Nicholas will come and see me when I'm finished?'

'Dr Nicholas will see you now,' said the unmistakable voice of the doctor from the doorway.

Both Penny and Jess protested. 'No! Not yet, Dr Nicholas. When Penny's finished. I don't want——' Jess began, only to be interrupted.

'All right, all right! I won't look. I'll stand behind you and watch Sister Anderson instead.'

If there was anything more likely to ensure that she make a mess of things than that, Penny reflected, she couldn't think what it was. A deep flush spread through her cheeks as she bent to her task again, and her hand shook. She tried not to think of him, and concentrated instead on applying the last touch of lipstick to Jessica's little mouth, and just a little mascara to her lashes. She bent forward to do it, smiling a little at the glow in Jessie's eyes, though she herself was still uneasily aware of Nicholas Adams' tall, powerful form propped against the wall a few feet away.

Finally she was finished. 'There!' she declared, straightening up to view the whole effect, and Nicholas Adams made a move to come and look, too.

'No!' cried Penny. 'Not yet! She's got to have her hair brushed.' Enthusiastically she reached for the brush and began to brush Jessie's restored curls around her face.

She felt rather than saw Adams' eyes on her face.

'It seems to me,' his deep voice said, 'that you're enjoying this as much as Jess.'

Penny concentrated on Jess's hair. 'Oh, I love putting on make-up,' she answered casually.

'But you don't wear any, Penny!' Jess objected.

Penny gave her a rueful look. 'Oh, well, I can't, you see,' she explained. 'The first thing I do is rub my face, and then it gets all over the place. I just can't stop myself.'

'Ooh, yes. I'll have to be careful of that,' said Jessica.

'Could I possibly have a look now?' asked Adams, and managed quite well the injured tone of one who has been forgotten.

Penny had to smile.

'Ready, Penny?' asked the girl.

'Ready,' pronounced Penny, and Nicholas Adams stepped forwards.

Penny hoped he would be diplomatic. The make-up she had used had been applied sparingly and skilfully enough, but Jessie still looked a little too young for it. She still had the round, soft face of a child, and the make-up, Penny thought, rather accentuated it.

Adams' response, however, was all Penny could have wished. He stood gazing at Jessica for a moment, looking very serious, which made Jess giggle.

'Why, Jessie,' he said softly. 'You look absolutely beautiful.'

Jessica giggled again, and clapped her hands.

'Do I?' she exclaimed delightedly. 'Do I really?'

'You certainly do,' the unit director declared solemnly. 'Why, if I were ten years younger. . .'

Penny reflected that it would have to be nearer to twenty years, but she didn't say so. She was smiling at Jessica's joy.

'Well, I wish you were,' said Jess ingenuously, 'because it would be nice to have a boyfriend and to be able to go on a date.'

Her voice was wistful, and Penny felt sorry for her

again. All dressed up, she thought, and nowhere to go.

Nicholas Adams might almost have thought of the old saying, too.

'Well,' he said slowly, 'I know I'm preposterously old, but I would be delighted if you would consider having a date with me.'

Penny felt her eyes drawn to him. How kind, was her one thought.

Jessica had drawn in her breath and looked at Penny.

'Oh, could I?' she asked. 'I'd love to go on a date with you, Dr Nicholas. And I don't mind you being old at all,' the twelve-year-old girl said kindly to the heart-throb of a hundred nurses. 'Where would we go?'

'Well. . .' said Dr Nicholas, and appeared to be stumped. 'Where do you suggest, Sister Anderson? I don't really know where young ladies like to go these days. I've got out of the way of it.'

Penny thought.

'Perhaps the pictures?' she suggested and hoped he meant to go outside the hospital. Surely it would not hurt for Jessie to go just once, with her doctor along with her.

But he seemed to find the idea suitable.

'Miss Brand,' he said formally. 'Would you do me the honour of going to the pictures with me?'

'Oh, yes!' cried Jess, delighted at the turn events had taken. 'We could see *Superman*! That is——' She hesitated. 'Would you like to see *Superman*, Dr Nicholas?'

'Oh, yes,' Dr Nicholas assured her quickly, and with

admirable fortitude. 'I've been wanting to see *Superman* for a long time.'

Penny bent over to pack up Jessie's make-up and to hide the grin which she could not banish from her face. She managed not to laugh.

That evening, travelling home on the bus, Penny relived the scene in her mind, and found it made her smile anew. What a lovely thing for Jess. And what a lovely thing to do, she thought. Her face softened as she remembered his tact and kindness.

Blast him, she thought. Why can't he be consistent? Either all bad, or all good? Even as she thought it, she knew it was ridiculous. No one was.

But the fact remained that Penny Anderson really didn't know what to make of the unit head, or how she should feel about him.

CHAPTER EIGHT

IT DIDN'T take long for the day of Jess and Nicholas's 'date' to come round.

And Penny, helping Jess to get ready, couldn't decide whether she wanted most to laugh or to cry. It meant so much to the little girl—not going out with Nicholas so much, but going out with someone.

'Penny,' she whispered, 'do you think he'll kiss me goodnght?'

Penny smiled. She thought of Nicholas Adams, and hoped very hard he would. Somehow she thought he might. This situation was going to call for great sensitivity on his part, but she thought where children were concerned he had it.

'He might, Jess,' she replied. 'Would you like him to?'

'Just once,' she said. 'To see what it's like.'

They both grinned.

Jess had a new dress. Her mother had bought it, but Penny had gone out in her lunch-hour to help her choose. It was hard for her mother not to see her child as a baby still, and it had to be a dress for a teenager.

Jess loved it. She paraded slowly before Penny after Penny had finished her make-up. Her hair was tucked up with a tortoise-shell comb. Her eyes shone with joy.

Penny was glad that Nicholas had come at that moment. Her feelings had threatened to engulf her.

And she forgot them momentarily when she saw him. He was wearing a navy blue sports jacket that seemed moulded to his broad shoulders, and a fresh white shirt and light grey trousers. He looked wonderful.

Penny felt a strange feeling of warmth and tension creep through her. I'm as excited for Jess as she is herself, she thought.

'I want a photograph of my girl,' he announced, and held up his camera. 'May I, Jess?'

Jess was delighted.

'Now the two of you, Sister Anderson?' he told her when he had taken one of Jess.

Shyly, Penny stepped in front of the camera and the two girls hugged each other as he pressed the button.

'Shall I take one of you, Dr Adams?' Penny asked.

'No, Sister,' he said gravely. 'It's a very expensive camera.'

Jess laughed delightedly, and, laughing herself, Penny left them.

What a special thing it is we share with these children, Penny thought to herself as she curled up in bed that night. And how blessed that there are people like Adams to do what he's doing for Jess. She thought of him again as he'd been that afternoon. What a strange man—so harsh, so kind.

She drifted into sleep, and dreamed of Jess and Nicholas Adams. They were dancing in a glittering ballroom, and then he was kissing Jess goodnight. Only suddenly it wasn't Jess. Strangely, disturbingly, it was her, and she could feel his lips turning her to fire and her body melting against him. . .

Penny jerked awake, gasping. She remembered the

dream. It was as clear as reality, and her heart was still hammering as it had been in her dream. What a funny trick for her unconsciousness to play.

Penny rolled over in bed and made the pillow a more comfortable shape. She lay there still feeling her heart beating. Oh, well, she yawned. It didn't matter. But it was still some time before the tension seemed to leave her and she drifted off again.

In the morning Penny went straight to see Jess. She knew from her own teenage years that half the fun lay in the telling. She was right.

'Oh, Penny, it was wonderful. I had such a wonderful time. He was so nice, and funny.' The little girl's eyes were shining. 'And I loved *Superman*.'

'Are you tired?' asked Penny, and Jessie wrinkled her nose.

'Don't tell anyone else. Yes, I am, but I don't care, Penny.'

Penny understood. 'Tell me what else,' she urged.

'Well. . .' Jess smiled shyly, and whispered, 'He kissed me goodnight.'

And they both giggled.

Well done, thought Penny. Well done, Nicholas.

'It was nice,' said Jess, 'but funny.'

This made Penny laugh even more. She wondered how Dr Adams would feel to know that being kissed by him felt 'funny'.

It was the morning of the unit meeting. Nicholas Adams was there when she arrived, and they exchanged a smile as Penny took her chair. Whatever this man did now, thought Penny, she would always be grateful to him for his kindness to Jess.

She studied his face as he spoke to his neighbour,

Dr Langley. The lines of brow, nose and jaw were strong and uncompromising, but his mouth was a softening influence. It was humorous, and most wonderfully shaped, Penny thought—at least, it was when he wasn't being grim.

And, as she studied it, her dream came back to her with a force and clarity that was unexpected. She felt it again—that mouth, moving on hers in a slow, sensuous incendiary motion. Her breath seemed to strangle in her throat.

'Are you all right, Pen?' asked Jeanna Wallace, and Penny was jerked back to the present.

'Y-yes,' she stumbled. 'I'm fine.'

'Are you unwell? You sort of went white then pink, just then.'

Penny managed to laugh. 'No, honestly, Jeanna. I'm all right. I was just thinking of something I'd forgotten.'

The meeting had begun, but Penny had trouble concentrating on it. She was profoundly disturbed by her thoughts and feelings. She'd never experienced anything like it before. She wondered what it meant, whether it meant anything. Nicholas Adams was very attractive. Perhaps it wasn't abnormal to have such thoughts about an attractive man. Or perhaps it was only triggered off by her dream—a dream that was a random collection of images, thrown together without sense. Dreams didn't really mean anything. . .

It was at this point in her deliberations that Jeanna dug her in the ribs and she looked up. Nicholas Adams was addressing her.

'Sister Anderson,' he said gently. 'Hello.'

She blushed. 'I'm sorry, Dr Adams, were you speaking to me?'

'At some length,' he replied wryly.

'I'm sorry,' she said again. 'I was thinking.' She saw that half-smile curve his lips.

'Evidently an absorbing occupation,' he commented, and a few people laughed.

She smiled sheepishly herself, feeling very foolish.

'We have been discussing the case of Sarah Williams,' he continued. 'Have you heard any of it, Sister Anderson?'

Penny was relieved that she knew something of Sarah's case. She was a child of eleven who had been referred here for tests. Everyone had been at a loss to explain her terrible temper tantrums and bad behaviour, and the psychiatrist she had seen had finally admitted her here for examination. It was possible, they thought, that she had a tumour or some other cerebral problem.

'She is going to require special handling,' Dr Adams was saying. 'She'll be my patient, and I think you can help me with her.'

Penny was glad he thought so, but secretly doubted it. She had no great opinion of her own abilities. She was happy, however, to try.

It proved very time-consuming. Performing tests on the child was difficult, since she was angry and uncooperative. Adams seemed anxious not to press the girl too far, and Penny realised why when one of the nurses antagonised her. Sarah flew into a rage and had to be physically restrained. They had not been able to stop her soon enough. She had broken a window and hit one of the other children first.

Berensen was furious. 'The kid shouldn't be here,' she snarled, well within Sarah's listening range. 'They should take her to a mental hospital.'

Penny was appalled. It was true in a way. The child was dangerous. But what sort of treatment for a possible tumour would she get in a mental hospital? And how could Berensen make such a statement in her hearing?

She wondered what to do. Dr Adams would be coming back to do an EEG on her at four-thirty. They had to calm her down by then.

Penny went to sit beside her. The child was a sorry sight. They had put restraints on her, and she lay trapped in her bed, only her eyes moving feverishly in her pale face over the objects around her. She looked like a little girl possessed, and Penny shivered. She tried to talk to her. Sarah snarled at Penny in response. Penny began again, and Sarah spat at her. With her heart sinking, Penny tried to imagine what it must be like to be Sarah at this moment. It must be horrible. And frightening. Perhaps frightening, most of all.

She voiced her thought. 'Are you very frightened, Sarah?' she asked gently.

Sarah looked at her a moment, and seemed suddenly to be on the brink of tears. But Dr Adams had come in, and Sarah recovered herself.

'I hate you!' she said to Penny. 'I want you to die.'

As Dr Adams came to stand on the other side of the bed, Penny got up from her chair.

'I'm sorry you hate me, Sarah,' she said sadly, and began to walk away. She had only gone three steps when she heard the child's cry.

'Don't go!' it came, in a wail.

They managed to get the EEG done that evening by six o'clock and, because Sarah was being reasonably co-operative with Penny standing by her side, they took her up for a brain scan as well.

It was eight o'clock by the time they had finished. Dr Adams had told Penny that she must go if she wanted, but she knew he wanted her to stay, and she could not have considered leaving Sarah while she seemed to be of some use.

But at ten-past eight they could finally leave her in the care of the night staff, and Penny could go. She collected her bag from her office, and walked to the lift to find Adams standing there still.

'It's been a long day for you,' he said. 'I'm grateful you stayed. I would never have got those tests done without you.'

'Oh,' replied Penny, 'I don't mind. I'm glad if I was some help.'

Penny was a muddle of emotions and thoughts. On the one hand, she remembered her thoughts and feelings of this morning only too well. She had spent the last four hours with him, and she felt an almost desperate need to get away and think about things.

On the other hand, how nice of him to wait and thank her. And she wanted somehow to thank him for what he'd done for Jess. He probably knew how much it meant but, if he didn't, he ought to.

'Dr Adams——' Penny raised her eyes to his face '——you made Jess very happy,' she said simply.

He stood looking down at her for what seemed like a small eternity. Then, very slowly, he raised a hand and gently lifted a lock of hair from her face and tucked it behind her ear. His hand stayed there, one silken strand between his fingers.

Penny had stopped breathing. She could not move her eyes from his face. She could not begin to interpret the look there.

The lift stopped noisily and the doors opened. He dropped his hand.

'I'm glad she's happy,' he merely replied, but his voice was low and gruff and strangely constricted.

Penny seemed to stumble into the lift. She would have liked to have been able to find something light to say on the way down, but she could think of nothing, so they rode in silence. When they reached the ground floor, they walked as silently through the foyer together, Adams holding the door open for her to go out.

'Can I give you a lift?' he asked.

Hastily, she shook her head. 'No, thank you. I'm— OK.'

He nodded. 'Goodnight, Penny,' he said, and gave her a small, strange smile before striding away to where the senior doctors parked their cars.

It seemed to Penny as she walked down to the bus stop that she was only now beginning to breathe again. What—what a funny thing to do, was her only thought. And how it had disconcerted her. Then she saw the bus, and was glad to relieve the tumult in her with a good sprint across the hospital lawn.

Carrie had eaten, so Penny tipped some baked beans into a saucepan, and her friend made a pot of tea while she ate them.

'How was your day?' Carrie asked.

'Mm,' said Penny vaguely, 'OK.'

There was a small silence, at the end of which Carrie set her cup on the table and folded her arms.

'Penelope,' she said, 'out with it.'

Penny gave a rueful smile. 'You know me well, don't you, Carrie?'

'Yep,' confirmed her friend.

Penny tok a sip of her tea, and a deep breath.

'Something—funny—happened this evening,' she began.

Carrie waited.

'It's hard to explain.'

'Try,' said Carrie.

'Well, maybe it goes back to last night, actually. Or—maybe that's got nothing to do with it.'

'Ye-e-s,' said Carrie helpfully.

It made Penny laugh, and that made her feel better.

'I had a dream about Adams.'

Carrie waited a moment, but Penny didn't go on. 'Nice dream? Nasty dream?' she asked finally.

'Well. . .' Penny wrinkled her brow. 'I suppose you'd say it was nice. . .'

'Go on,' said Carrie. She had sat up straighter.

'It made me feel a little strange with him today,' Penny went on. 'And then—tonight—we were waiting for the lift. He—waited for me. I'd helped him with something. He—was strange. He tucked my hair behind my ear. I guess it was a friendly gesture. You know—he was kind to me when I got dizzy. He stroked my head and took my pulse. But then he was being a doctor. This was—different. Well, friendly, I guess. That was OK. But—it was the way I felt. . .'

Carrie seemed to ask an entirely irrelevant question.

'What colour eyes has Adams got?'

'Grey, why?' answered Penny, surprised.

'What side of his head does he part his hair on?'

'W-What?' Penny stammered. 'What's that got to do with it? He—he doesn't part it. He sort of brushes it back.'

Carrie was grinning now. 'What colour eyes has Larry got?' she continued.

Penny looked at her friend as though she'd gone slightly mad.

'I don't know—blue, I think. Or green.'

'You've had dinner with him several times,' Carrie reminded her.

'Well, yes,' said Penny, with an air of some bewilderment.

'Then what colour eyes has he got?'

'I don't know,' Penny admitted. 'I can't remember.'

'Really?' said Carrie, with her eyebrows arched, and Penny sat suddenly silent.

'Has Adams ever smiled at you?' Carrie asked.

'Yes,' Penny answered.

'How did you feel?'

Penny sat looking at her friend, a slow flush spreading over her face.

'Oh, Carrie,' she groaned. 'Oh, Carrie.'

'I'm sorry, love,' Carrie answered. 'You have the symptoms of a rather serious disease. You're falling in love.'

And now that it had been said, Penny knew it was useless to deny it. A number of recollections came to her mind to confirm the diagnosis—the way she had felt when he came to take Jess out, the feeling of his eyes on her face, and that delicious disturbing dream.

It seemed such a short time ago that she had thoroughly disliked him. She had been so angry with him. And even a few days back she couldn't have said for sure that she liked him. She had found him too awe-inspiring to think of him as a man. A few short weeks ago she had thought Larry was silly to warn her not to get fond of Nicholas Adams.

How had it happened? When had it started? When she had seen him looking so wonderful for his date with Jess? No. Before then.

When he had come to see Jess in her make-up, and been so kind? Or even before then?

When he had asked her that strange question in his office? Perhaps.

She had noticed so many things about him that day. And so little about herself, she thought ruefully. The wonderful curve of his mouth, the way that his eyes alone could soften and smile, the strong arms and beautiful hands—she had noticed all those, and responded to them. But she had shut her eyes to her own response. She had called it something else. He intimidates me, she had said. He disconcerts me, unnerves me.

But now it had to be admitted—the truth about that odd, breathless feeling, the sweetly painful tightness in her chest, her hammering heart.

'Oh, no!' she groaned, and said to Carrie, 'What are you smiling at?'

'It had to happen some time,' said her friend. 'What's the problem? It sounds as though he's keen on you, too.'

'Oh, no! He couldn't be, Carrie! You should see the sister who's been pursuing him. She's stunning.'

'And not very pleased with you, it would seem,' replied Carrie meaningfully. 'Perhaps she's noticed how human the man of steel seems to be where you're concerned.'

'Oh no, Carrie! You couldn't—he just——'

Carrie was laughing. 'Oh, dear,' she said. 'Is it so inconceivable that someone like him should care for you, Penny?'

'Yes,' Penny answered truthfully. She couldn't conceive of it.

'You do have a problem with authority. He's only a man, Penny.'

Slowly, Penny shook her head. 'No, he's not "only a man", Carrie. You don't know Nicholas Adams. . .'

CHAPTER NINE

THE next morning Penny was able to view the whole situation a little more calmly.

Perhaps it wasn't quite as bad as falling in love, she told herself. What she had was a crush, just like the crushes girls get on doctors and teachers and even parsons—in fact, anyone out of their reach. She had a crush on her boss, who just happened to be brilliant and charming and handsome. It wasn't unusual. And it need go no further if she was careful to exercise control over herself.

Penny was even more convinced this morning that Adams could have no interest in such an insignificant part of the hospital hierarchy as herself. There must be dozens of quite eminent female doctors for a man like him to choose from! She kept trying not to think of his tucking her hair behind her ear, and failed. Finally she told herself that it would be a very big mistake for a very junior sister to read more into this than a 'thank you' for her help.

By dint of speaking to herself thus, Penny was able to show up at work that morning with a tolerable degree of composure.

It was very soon needed. It wasn't long before Nicholas Adams approached her on the ward to tell her the results of Sarah's tests.

'There's a tumour, all right,' he said. 'In the frontal

lobe, as expected from her tantrums. I'm almost sure from its form that it's operable.'

'That's good news!' said Penny.

'Yes,' said the doctor. 'As long as it's right. Anyway, we'll have to go in and see. And we'll have to convince Sarah to be co-operative.'

Penny saw that this would be no easy task. Brain scans were one thing, brain surgery was quite another.

Adams interrupted her thoughts. 'I hate to land this on you, but if anyone can do that I believe it's you.'

She tried to stop herself feeling absurdly pleased at the compliment.

Sarah went to Theatre round lunchtime. In the event, it was easier than either had expected. Sarah seemed relieved to know what was wrong with her, and consented to be good if only Penny would be with her when she went to sleep and woke up.

It seemed a very short time before she was called back to Theatre.

It was Adams himself on the phone.

'It was remarkably straightforward,' he told her. 'I'm confident we've got it all with the minimum of trauma to brain tissue.'

'Nicholas, that's wonderful!' exclaimed Penny, then blushed in mortification at her involuntary use of his first name.

But he only said, 'Yes, it's nice to win one, isn't it, Penny?' and they broke off.

Penny was with Sarah within a few minutes. The girl was in the recovery-room, not yet awake. Penny called her name a few times, and finally she opened her eyes.

'Penny?' she said faintly, and Penny answered.

'Yes, Sarah. I'm here. And you're all right. You're going to be just fine. Everything went wonderfully.'

Sarah gave the ghost of a smile. 'I'm sleepy,' she said. She closed her eyes again.

'OK,' said Penny. 'Go to sleep. And don't worry any more. I'll see you in the morning.'

'OK,' replied Sarah faintly, and Penny knew she could leave.

Outside Recovery, Penny found Nicholas Adams. He had changed from his theatre clothes and was leaning against the now deserted enquiry desk. He straightened up when he saw her, and smiled.

Penny smiled back. 'She seems fine,' she commented.

Nicholas Adams nodded. 'You, on the other hand, look tired and hungry. I should think your friend must have given up on you by now, and given your dinner to the cat.'

Penny laughed. 'There's always baked beans,' she said.

He grimaced. 'I couldn't have that on my conscience. I appreciate your staying—more than I can say. Let me buy you dinner.'

Penny felt flustered. 'Oh—I—Dr Adams—you don't have to do that. I was happy to stay.' She knew she was blushing.

He didn't seem to notice it. 'I know you were,' he said, 'and I appreciate that as much as the fact that you stayed.' He came to stand beside her. 'Come,' he coaxed her. 'I can't have you dining on baked beans. You're too valuable. There's a place in the Avenue that does excellent steaks. We'll go there.'

There didn't seem to be a way to refuse. In a kind

of trance, Penny walked beside him to the lift. She listened to his account of the operation as they rode down and walked out to his car, but took very little of it in.

Only in the cold air of the car park did her mind seem to clear, and she asked herself what she was doing. She ought to be keeping her distance, not accepting dinner invitations, however kindly meant.

'I hope you'll excuse the state of this ancient vehicle,' he was saying. 'I bought it when I passed my surgical primary. Somehow I haven't been able to bring myself to part with it.'

Penny smiled, surveying the somewhat battered Mercedes. 'I like it,' she said. 'It's friendly.'

For the first time, she heard him laugh out loud as he opened the door for her. 'Most of the time,' he agreed, 'but it has the occasional bout of ill-humour.'

Like you, Penny thought, as he got in beside her. 'What do you do then?' she asked instead.

'Curse it roundly and call a cab,' he replied with a smile.

Penny had never been to this place before. It was small and informal—the sort of place where you could relax, and where the food was plain but good. She sank back gratefully into her chair, and realised only then how tired she was. Before she had known it she had sighed aloud. She saw Nicholas Adams glance at her quickly.

'You're tired,' he observed.

She shook her head. How could she admit to tiredness when he had been working day and night? How did he do it? she wondered. Her eyes covertly searched his face. He looked better now. The tension was gone.

There were shadows still under his eyes, but it was a calm, strong, beautiful face before her.

Nicholas Adams' eyes flicked up from his menu and caught hers. They were clear, piercing grey in the candlelight, the pupils large. They met hers and stayed there.

Penny felt a clutch at her heart, and the same sweet, painful tightness in her throat and chest that she had known before. She should never have come. This was no way to cure a crush on the boss. Shaken, she dropped her eyes to her own menu, but it was a full minute before she could read the words that were printed there. The first drink helped. She felt some of her tension ebbing away as she finished it. And Nicholas Adams helped as well. He talked of the unit, of the things that interested them both. After a while she found she could reply intelligently. She told him more about the nurses' meetings, about the problems and concerns that were aired.

A small frown creased his brow. 'I've neglected that,' he said.

Penny gave him a smile. 'You can't do everything,' she replied. 'And if you did, what would I do?'

What Penny was coming to think of as 'that smile' spread across his face. Tonight it reached his eyes and lit them. And its effect on her made her hastily promise herself that she would never do this again. In future she would abide by her decision, and see as little as possible of Nicholas Adams.

'What do you do for recreation?' he asked suddenly.

'Oh—I sail as much as I can,' she told him.

'Do you? What do you sail?'

'Dinghies, Mirrors, Lasers. Whatever I can get my hands on. My friend—Carrie—comes too.'

'I used to do a bit of that,' he said quietly.

'What did you sail?' she asked.

'I have a little cutter. She's sitting on the mooring, rotting away.' There was a note of sadness in his voice.

'Oh, no!' Penny cried. 'Can't you—don't you have time?'

He gave a wry smile. 'I suppose I could make time. I should make time. Only——' he shrugged '—it's easy to let the ward absorb one's spare hours. And I don't have a Carrie to encourage me.'

He glanced up, his eyes smiling.

Penny nodded. 'It does help—having someone else who's interested.'

There was a long silence, during which Penny was uncomfortably aware of his eyes on her still. Then finally he spoke, and it was, for Nicholas Adams, an oddly halting speech.

'If you would like to come some time. . . She's a nice little boat. . . Or, if you prefer. . .you could take her out with your friend. She's just rotting away. She should be sailed.'

Penny stared at him, her eyes wide for a moment. He had invited her to sail with him. She didn't know what to say. A heady feeling of pleasure swept over her as she contemplated it. But she knew she couldn't—shouldn't—do it.

Nor, in common politeness, could she say she would prefer to take his boat out with her friend. A pang of regret seized her.

She groped for a non-committal reply. 'Th-that's awfully kind,' she managed. 'I—perhaps when things get less busy. . . Thank you for the offer. It's very kind. You don't even know what kind of sailor I am.'

Nicholas Adams didn't reply at once. Then finally he gave a smile that seemed to Penny a little sad.

'Let me know if you want her,' he said briefly, and turned his eyes once more to his plate.

As she had with Larry, Penny offered to take the bus home when the time came to go. But Nicholas Adams wasn't Larry. He gave her a faintly incredulous glance, said, 'You certainly won't,' and firmly steered her towards the car. And, in contrast to her experience with Larry, Penny felt unable to resist.

Moreover, he did not say in the car when they reached her house. In a moment Nicholas had climbed out and taken her arm with the obvious intention of escorting her to the door.

In the midst of the confusion that his hand on her arm seemed to cause her, Penny wondered whether she should invite him in for coffee. But his words answered her.

'We both need some sleep,' he said. 'Make sure you don't sit up writing reports.

Penny gave a nervous chuckle. 'I won't,' she promised. She turned to him on the doorstep, intending to thank him, and found her mouth rather dry. 'Thank you, Dr Adams,' she said. 'You didn't have to do that. I want to be useful to the ward. B-but—I enjoyed it. Thanks.'

He stood there looking down at her, his hand still clasped quite firmly on her arm. She couldn't see his face. It was in shadow. But she felt him give her arm the faintest squeeze.

'My pleasure,' he murmured in a low, gruff voice,

and in a moment had released her, turned on his heel, and strode off down the path.

Penny let herself in, shut the door behind her, and leaned against it. 'Carrie. . .' she called in a soft little wail, and bit her lip.

Penny sighed at the pile of files on her desk, and took Jessica Brand's off the top. It was fortunate that Nicholas Adams had taken Jess out on their date when he had, for they had become extraordinarily busy again. She was beginning to get used to the ebb and flow—the weeks that were bearable and the weeks that were bedlam.

She was glad to see very little of any of the doctors for a while. As always in their busy times, she saw more of Larry than Nicholas.

Larry continued to seek her company, and to try to persuade her to have dinner with him again. She was friendly towards him, and enjoyed his humour, but she was less inclined to go out with him than ever. She tried to convince herself that this had nothing to do with Nicholas, and almost succeeded.

She did all she could to help on the ward, and regularly gave out the pain-killers now, and some other drugs, too. All the spare time she could find, she spent with Jess.

They talked about Penny's teenage years—boyfriends she had had and dates she had been on.

Jessica was living her life to some extent through Penny, and Penny was glad to have it so, knowing that Jessie had only a very little left of her own. She told her all she wanted to know.

'Have you ever been in love?' Jess asked her.

Penny wrinkled her brow. 'Well, no. Not really. I don't think so. I thought I was a couple of times when I was sixteen or seventeen, but I wasn't really.'

'How did you know you weren't really?' pursued the child.

'Well, because I forgot about them when somebody else came along. Once I forgot about one of them when my father gave me a pony. I don't think that happens if you're really in love,' Penny told her.

'Are you in love now?' Jessica asked.

Penny wondered where Dr Adams was at this moment. She had seen him come into the ward. She answered quickly. 'No, not at the moment, I'm not.'

Jessica looked disappointed. 'Not even a little bit?'

'No, not the littlest bit right now.'

'Not with Dr Larry?'

Penny was firm. 'Certainly not with Dr Larry.'

'I wish you would fall in love,' said Jessica. 'Then you could tell me all about it.'

Penny felt mean for lying. She knew she *was* in love a little bit. And she wouldn't have minded telling Jess. The child could keep a secret. It was just that the person she was 'a little bit' in love with could well be within earshot.

He was. Dr Adams was standing closeted by screens at the next bed, inspecting a wound with apparent concentration. He couldn't have failed to hear, however, every word that had passed between Jessica and Penny. He began to hum as he applied the new dressing himself. Dr Adams seemed in a very good mood today, thought Staff Nurse Drew.

* * *

Over the next days things were worse for the surgeons. There were new patients, and some old ones with complications—things they could have done without.

Penny watched the ward staff with interest, anxious to see whether their lunchtime meeting was making any difference. She thought it was. They seemed more able to work together than before.

And, at the next meeting, they agreed it was so.

'It's a pity you can't do something to help the doctors cope, Pen,' remarked Janet Drew. 'It's so much worse for them than us.'

She knew it was so. She had seen Dr Adams that day, and he looked as he had on that occasion weeks ago when he'd exploded at Veronica Lang.

She nodded sadly.

'Adams is back to no sleep,' said Janet. 'And that kid he did last night is going to have to go back to Theatre. His pressure's rising.'

Penny knew what it meant. The painstaking installation of a shunt to keep the pressure in his brain down.

'There should be another unit. We shouldn't be the only one in a city this size.'

They all agreed.

And Penny felt sorry for them all, especially Nicholas. She could no longer allow herself to feel glad that the work was keeping him away from her. No one should have to give as much of himself as he did.

It was six o'clock when Penny finished arranging accommodation at a hotel near by for a bewildered country couple whose child was in the unit.

She heard the knock at her door, and thought, Damn. That's Larry.

She was wrong. It was Adams. And tonight he looked more exhausted than she had ever seen him. He looked ready to drop.

'Come in,' she said hastily, and pulled him out a chair. Gratefully he sank into it.

There was a wild look about him. If he had shaved that morning, it hadn't been very thorough, and he had obviously pulled his theatre cap off without bothering to comb his tousled hair. He was still in theatre pyjamas.

Penny waited for him to say what he wanted, but he didn't say anything at all. So she asked him if he would like some tea.

'That would be nice,' he said, smiling faintly.

She made him some, and put it beside him with the tin of biscuits that she kept for families and tried not to eat herself.

He seemed to have nothing to say. He simply sat slumped in the chair, staring at the ground before him.

Penny suddenly felt a rush of pity, and her nervousness seemed to melt away. She couldn't see him as 'Authority' now, or as the doctor whom her crush had made dangerous to her. She only saw him as a man— dedicated, dogged, exhausted.

She wanted to help him.

'How did it go?' she asked gently.

He looked up at her. 'Oh, some we win,' he said with infinite tiredness, 'and others. . .' He shook his head. 'How much longer before my nurses pass out on the theatre floor?'

He seemed to be almost talking to himself.

Penny got up and poured him more tea. She stood beside his chair for a moment.

'How much longer before *you* do?' she asked softly.

He looked up at her, and all at once, before Penny knew what was happening, he sat forward, reached out his arms and pulled her against him.

He held her hard, his face against her. She heard him say her name in an agonised whisper.

And, in the feelings that flooded her now, Penny Anderson knew that this was no crush. She longed to hold him forever, to stroke his hair and say his name, and smooth away his exhaustion and his pain. She loved him.

Instinctively her arms had gone about him, and she let them stay there, hoping they would make him feel at least that someone cared.

She realised that her heart was knocking against her ribs, and hoped he couldn't feel it. She made a move as though to draw back just a little, but his arms gripped her more tightly.

She gave in to the man's need for closeness, and her own. She let her body relax against his, feeling his warmth and his hardness with an acuteness that made her throat ache. And gradually she felt his tension decrease, and the arms that held her fiercely became caressingly gentle.

It seemed to Penny that they stayed there for an eternity. And then he moved back from her, still holding her, and raised his face to hers. It held an expression of painful intensity. He opened his mouth to speak, when a knock sounded at the door.

He didn't move for a moment. But the knock came again, more loudly, and slowly he released her.

Penny went to answer it. It was Berensen.

'Is Dr Adams here?' she asked. 'Drew said——'

'What is it?' he asked shortly.

'Oh, Dr Adams. . .' Berensen was stiffly polite. 'I'm sorry to disturb you, but I think that shunt's blocked.'

Nicholas only sighed. 'OK,' he said. 'I'm coming.'

And, amazingly, he turned to Penny in front of Berensen, and reached out to squeeze her hand. 'Thanks,' he said softly, and was gone.

Penny spoke to her family once a week. There were still five Anderson children at home, and that made long-distance phone calls expensive. She had to speak to seven people.

'It sounds as though you're doing all you can to help,' her father was saying.

'Yes, I am, I suppose,' Penny said doubtfully. 'But I feel so sorry for them. I wish there was more I could do. Especially for Nicholas Adams. He bears the brunt of the strain.'

'He sounds a very fine man,' said her father.

'Yes,' she agreed. 'He is.'

As Penny hung up the receiver she reflected how much her opinions had changed. If her father had said that a month ago, she wouldn't have told him that. She had to smile at herself, even though it hurt as well. She loved Nicholas so much now, with a passion she knew was both physical and mental. She admired him, respected him, but she had also thrilled to his touch, to the feel of his arms around her, and the meeting of their eyes.

What was she to make of this evening? One thing she knew—she had seen the real Nicholas Adams at last. This was no machine. This was a man—a human being—tired, troubled, in need of comfort. And this was a man who felt things. Penny was sure of that now. Perhaps even a man who felt things more deeply than most, and whose cool and sometimes harsh veneer was a defence against those feelings.

Penny felt a wave of love and longing flood her. Had Nicholas Adams remained as he was, her feelings might never have amounted to more than a crush, she thought. Impossible to feel real love for a figure-head, a façade. But now a real man had reached out to her, and her heart had answered.

What did it mean, that reaching out? Penny's heart beat fast at the question she asked herself. Could it possibly mean that he cared? It must surely mean that he liked her, trusted her, at least.

Penny frowned. She had to be very careful. She mustn't let her imagination run away with her, her own wishes obscure reality. She had a sympathetic face, Larry had said. Nicholas Adams had been near to exhaustion. She had offered him comfort, and he had taken it. Like a small boy, he had hugged her—not like a lover, she warned herself. He had thanked her for her sympathy. She mustn't read any more into things than that. Perhaps it meant they were friends at last, but it couldn't be anything more. There was too wide a gulf between them.

And yet a small, stubborn hope took root in her, and she couldn't quite kill it off. She told herself it was dangerous. It persisted. She told herself they were worlds apart. It flourished still. She knew it was born of her own feelings, her longing that he might care, rather than of any objective reality. And she knew she wasn't the first to have felt it; but even so, it wouldn't go away.

CHAPTER TEN

OVER the next days it became harder than ever for Penny to contain that crazy hope. They were busy, as ever, but she seemed to see the unit director more often than before. Before Theatre and after, and in between cases, he was to be found on the ward, examining children, explaining things to their parents, and sometimes just sitting on the end of a bed, holding a small hand in his own.

His presence was acutely disturbing to Penny, and yet she longed to see him. She seemed to exist in a curious state of breathlessness, which became more acute when his tall form appeared on the ward, and threatened to overcome her completely when they came face to face.

For now his 'Good morning' was accompanied by a smile which reached into her heart and left it slamming against her ribs. She hardly knew what she replied to him, and had to wrench her eyes from the grey ones that scanned her face with such searching attention.

He seemed to feel the need to discuss the patients with her, surely more often than before, she thought. And Penny would endure the sweet agony of having him prop himself on the ward desk beside her, his strong, wonderful face looking down into her own.

They were speaking now of Sarah.

'I suppose it may leave scars on their relationships,' he was saying. 'She has been so difficult to handle for so long. Aggressive, verbally and physically. It must take even the most loving parents and siblings a while to get over the hurt of that.'

Penny was looking up at him. Slowly she shook her head. 'I don't think so,' she said softly. 'When you love someone it's easy to forgive them. You look for ways to excuse them. When they behave badly it hurts and grieves you, but you close your eyes as much as you can to the bad part, and search in them for the person you know is there, the person you love.'

Nicholas Adams looked down at her for a long moment, in which her heart appeared to suspend its normal function. His face held a curious tension, but it was his eyes which arrested Penny and made it impossible for her to look away. They were full of a soft, warm light that seemed to flood her in turn with warmth.

When, finally, he spoke, his voice was low and somehow constricted. 'I hope so,' was all he said, but he stayed where he was, his eyes locked on hers till Penny felt a flush suffuse her face.

She was almost glad when Berensen interrupted.

'You can see that boy now, if you like, Penny,' the sister said.

'Oh. Th-thanks,' Penny stammered.

Berensen flashed her a brilliant smile, which, Penny felt, owed more to the presence of Nicholas Adams than to any friendliness Berensen felt for her. Though, to be charitable, she had to admit that the charge sister had been much more polite and pleasant towards her lately than ever before.

It was curious. If anything, she had expected Belinda to be more hostile after finding Adams in her office

like that. But it hadn't happened that way at all, and
Penny was forced to take herself to task for her
negative thoughts about her. Perhaps she had misinter-
preted Belinda from the start. Perhaps Belinda, hard-
pressed like everyone else, had only resented the fact
that she wasn't a ward nurse—an extra pair of hands
for the clinical team. Now that she had shown herself
more than willing to help out with the clinical work
when necessary, Belinda had obviously begun to
accept her.

It was a view that Larry regarded with cynicism.

'Watch out for her,' he counselled. 'I'll admit she
cares about her work, and that she's very good at it.
But that isn't the only reason for her dislike of you,
my sweet. Knowing her as I do, I warn you that she
would be only too happy to put a spoke in your wheel.'

Penny made a wry face. 'You *are* dramatic, Doctor.
I don't see what she can do to me, anyway.'

'Anything she can think of to scupper the blossom-
ing—er—shall we say friendship between you and
Nicholas Adams, dearest girl?'

Penny's head jerked up from her lunch. To her
annoyance, she felt her face begin to flame.

Before she could speak, Larry held up his hands and
laughed. 'OK, OK,' he said. 'I know. It's not true.
There's nothing in it. I'm imagining things.' He
grinned, but his face was a trifle tense, and his voice
had an edge to it. 'But if I am, so are many of our
colleagues, my sweet.'

'What do you mean?' she flung in dismay.

'Just that others have noticed that you and the boss
seem to have a lot to talk about lately, and that you
seem to be—er—the recipient of more friendliness on

the part of Nick than the rest of us. Not that you don't deserve it,' he added quickly. 'You *are* very special, my little friend. I've never met anyone like you. As wise as an old woman one moment, and an excited child the next. It's a winning combination, Penny. Especially coupled with the loveliest face in the world, and one which, I ought tell you, mirrors your every thought and feeling, my love.'

Penny's heart thudded. Oh, God. Had she given herself away? Had she been wearing her heart on her sleeve, for all to read? And, most embarrassing of all, for Nicholas Adams to read?

She took a deep breath. And yet, wasn't it true what Larry was saying? She had met Nicholas so often lately on the ward, and in Theatre. And never had he failed to look in her direction, to say a few words at least, and to give her that smile that did such odd things to her heart.

That wild, crazy hope leapt up in her. Hadn't his eyes been full of something soft and warm at times? Hadn't he lingered with her longer than was strictly necessary at times? Hadn't he worn an almost regretful air when called away?

With a great effort, Penny marshalled a semblance of calm. 'Larry, I don't want people reading things into a little friendliness,' she said.

He received her in silence.

Penny drew another breath. 'I do like Nicholas Adams. I like him a lot. And perhaps he likes me. But not one word, not one hint of anything more has ever passed between us. Do you understand?'

Penny saw Larry's mouth curve into a rather sardonic smile. 'Oh, I do understand,' he said in a low voice. It was also ineffably sad.

And she knew that Larry had a right to be sad, if indeed he did care for her. For she had lied to him. There *had* been a hint of something more. And, even if there hadn't, even if there never was anything more than friendship, Nicholas Adams had eclipsed Larry forever in her heart and mind, like the sun eclipses a pale and insipid moon.

That afternoon, she and Nicholas Adams met again, this time with the Brands, to discuss their plans for Jess.

Jess was going home. Or, if not precisely home, she was leaving the hospital for a while. An old school-friend of Mrs Brand lived only half an hour from the hospital, and she was going away for a month. The Brands were going to stay in her house, and take Jessie there with them. It would give them some time together in a normal environment, and yet be close enough to stay in contact with the hospital.

Jessie didn't seem to know at first whether to be delighted or sad but, when Penny promised to visit her at home, her ambivalence evaporated. Dr Nicholas was to see her there as well. Penny wondered how on earth he would fit it in, but knew that he would do it somehow.

Despite the fact that they would see each other still, Penny knew it would be hard for them to say goodbye when the day for Jess to leave arrived. They had seen each other every day in the ward, and now there would be a gap there.

And it only foreshadowed things to come, she thought, with a contraction at her heart.

Perhaps Nicholas Adams had seen that brief look of

pain in Penny's eyes, for he asked her to stay when the Brands had left.

And, indeed his words confirmed it.

'Penny, this is going to be very hard for you, I think,' he observed. 'You care about Jess very much.'

'Yes. I do,' she said, and gave a little smile.

'I don't want to see you hurting,' he stated simply, but the gruff sincerity of his tone touched her.

She shook her head. 'I'll hurt, when she—dies. But—I won't be crushed. I'm very strong. I've met with—loss—before, and I know that one must face the feelings that come, and that if one does, one recovers.' She looked up at him and smiled again, a small, sad smile.

He was regarding her intently, the suggestion of a frown on his face. 'I know you're strong. I have reason to know that. But this loss—this may reawaken old ones, you know.'

'I know that. It has already.'

'I have no right to ask—but. . .' Nicholas' voice faltered.

And Penny realised she trusted him now. For she didn't mind telling him about that other loss—about Meg, who'd been her special sister, and who had dwindled away before her eyes. And even when tears came she had no wish to hide them from the man who sat before her with a look of mingled pain and concern in his eyes.

'I still wish one could think of a reason why it happens,' she said at length. 'But I don't think there is one. It just happens. It's just life.'

He nodded. 'Yes,' he breathed. 'It has no purpose. Sometimes it makes people stronger and more caring, as it has you. But that's coincidental. There's no purpose in it at all.'

His voice was infinitely sad and weary. Without even thinking, Penny put her hand out and rested it on his arm in the same gesture she might have used with a parent.

And Nicholas Adams caught up her hand in his own and held it with a fierce pressure that surprised her. With a hasty movement, he turned towards her. 'Penny,' he said, and his voice was harsh and strained. 'This is—this is a terrible moment to try and tell you——' He broke off and looked at her fiercely, as though trying to gauge whether he ought continue.

And Penny, meeting his eyes, felt a shock buffet her as she recognised the naked hunger and longing that dwelt there.

He took a few ragged breaths, and covered her hand with his other one, so that it lay imprisoned in his clasp. 'You're so lovely,' he uttered in a tortured voice. 'So lovely, and warm, and alive.'

And in another moment he had leaned towards her, put one hand behind her head, and drawn her lips up to his.

Penny gave a gasp as they met, gently at first, with almost unbearable restraint. And then his slow exploratory movement on her mouth gave way to an urgent, demanding pressure that made all the emotions of her dream a reality. A sweet fire sprang up and began to rage in her. Her chest burned with it, and she struggled for breath.

The sound of his pager exploded between them, and Penny sprang back, her lips parted and face flushed.

Nicholas Adams, his eyes on her, gave a kind of

groan. With a savage movement he tore the thing from his belt and listened.

'Dr Adams wanted urgently in Theatre,' it said. He swore. Then abruptly he rose, still holding her hand, and pulled her up and against him. His arms went round her and crushed her yielding body against his muscular hardness. He only held her to him a moment. Then he had released her, met her eyes for an instant, and left without another word.

And if the feeling of him hadn't left Penny too weak to stand, the look in his eyes certainly had. They were wild, the grey darkened almost to black, and there burned in them an intensity of passion that Penny had never seen or imagined.

Penny collapsed back in her chair in the interview-room, and let her feelings wash over her. Her heart was hammering. She put her hands up to her face. It was flaming. Her breathing was as ragged as his had been.

He cared. He had called her lovely, and warm, and alive. He had kissed her. He had held her as though unwilling to let her go, then released her with pain. He wanted her. There was no doubt. And now she relaxed and let her joy well up in her. He cared. Miraculously, he cared. How much, and in what way, she didn't know. And she wasn't sure that it mattered.

It was a full half-hour before Penny Anderson had calmed herself enough to know that, to someone like her, it did matter. She sat in her chair and pondered it. Did he love her? She searched those cherished memories of all their meetings over the last few weeks. There was a warmth in him, a tenderness. But did that mean he loved her?

She recognised with a thrill, and almost a twinge of fear, that he desired her. She had felt that in his lips and his arms, and seen it on his face.

And if that was all, what then? Suddenly she was seized by doubt, and it was doubt of herself. Feeling as she did, what would happen if that was all his feelings amounted to? For all her background and beliefs, Penny could feel no assurance that she could ever withstand him.

He *must* love her, as she did him. She would will him to. And, as she thought again of the emotion in his face as she'd told him Meg's story, she was almost sure that it was so.

The day passed in a sort of haze. Mechanically she completed her tasks, but the only time she fully emerged from her preoccupation was when she heard someone say that Adams would be in Theatre till midnight.

She left at last and travelled home on the bus, staring through the window into the darkness outside, and saying to herself like a sort of chant, 'I love him. I love him. He must love me.'

The morning was beautiful—clear and sunlit. Penny's heart as she rode to work seemed to glide with the birds, dipping and wheeling over the park they passed on the way.

There was nothing to mar her soaring spirits.

The first Penny knew of the storm to break over her was the absence of Sister Berensen from the ward that morning. Penny had sought her to discuss moving Sarah into Jessie's old bed. It had a fine view over the hospital gardens, and though Sarah was recovering apace from her ordeal she was rather low in spirits. Penny felt the change would help her.

There was no warning presentiment in Penny when she was told that Berensen had gone to see the matron, either—she only felt faintly curious, and resolved to find her after lunch. And, even when a message came summoning Penny to the matron's office, it was only curiosity which stirred in her.

But, when she was shown into that lady's room, and found not only Matron there, but the assistant matron and Nicholas Adams as well, her curiosity turned to surprise. For a moment her heart leapt to see him. But then she noticed the grimness of the faces before her. Penny's first stirring of pleasure at the sight of him died at birth.

And at last she began to feel misgiving. What had happened?

The matron spoke. 'Sit down, please, Sister Anderson.'

Penny sat.

Matron seemed to search her face for an instant. 'Do you know why I've asked you here?' she enquired. Her tone was grave.

Penny shook her head and replied, 'No, Matron.' She glanced at Nicholas as if to divine from his face the reasons, but his head was bowed. For the first time, Penny felt the beginnings of alarm. And, in a moment, she knew it had been justified, for Matron was making the most incredible and most awful charge against her. It was calmly delivered, without indignation or anger, and even perhaps with sympathy. But the accusation was horrible. She was said to have stolen drugs.

Penny was stunned. Her face, in a moment, was ashen. Her mouth was dry. She could think of no word to say. Finally she merely shook her head, her heart pounding in her ears.

Matron regarded her intently. 'Do you deny it?' she asked.

Penny found her tongue. 'Yes!' was all she could say, but it was a cry of anguish.

Matron seemed to give the smallest sigh. 'I see,' she said, and seemed to sit thinking. But then she roused herself. 'The situation is this,' she said softly. 'Sister Berensen and Sister Douglas counted the narcotics and the tranquillisers yesterday evening as they normally do. The count did not agree with the drugs that had been recorded as given out. Now, the pharmacist only delivered the new supply at lunchtime yesterday, and I am told that you are the only one who took drugs from the supply in the afternoon.'

Wildly, Penny shook her head again. 'I gave them to a patient,' she cried. 'They were ordered!'

'Yes, we know you gave some to a patient, Sister Anderson, but there were more missing than you gave.'

The horror of it seemed to pervade Penny's very bones. Her limbs felt heavy and weak.

'Have you any explanation?' Matron was asking.

Penny racked her brain. Had she not put the bottle back? No, she knew she had. And she hadn't dropped any. She had carefully taken two tablets out and resealed the container. There was no mistake. She could think of no explanation, if no one else had gone to the cabinet. And it was always locked. She had locked it again and returned the key to Sister Berensen.

Her heart gave a lurch. Sister Berensen kept the keys. She had told Matron that no one else had used any drugs. But Sister Berensen could have.

Penny's mind was racing now. Sister Berensen disliked her. She always had. She cared for Nicholas Adams and had found him in her office, had seen him take her hand. . .

It was a preposterous thought. Impossible. No nurse would do that to another—willingly, malignantly. It would end her career. And yet, when the sister's face swam before her, it held a malicious sneer.

Could it have happened that way?

Penny looked up from her thoughts, her lips parted as if to speak. She looked at the faces of the women before her. They were waiting, concerned, almost sad.

They would never believe her. And how could she make the accusation, without any proof?

Immobilised by the horror of it, feeling as though it were a nightmare and she must soon wake up, Penny sat staring ahead of her. Her face still wore its deathlike pallor, her jaw clenched as if in pain.

She had not looked at Nicholas again. For the worst of the feelings that lacerated her now was the humiliation of being so accused before this man. But, even as the shame pierced her, and she willed herself to look straight ahead, she felt her eyes drawn to him.

Nicholas Adams also sat immobile in his chair. His face was turned away, his eyes on the floor. And now, perversely, Penny felt an overwhelming desire for him to look at her—to look up, to meet her eyes, to show in some small way that he didn't believe this. She stared at his face, half turned from her. Penny willed him to meet her gaze.

He kept his eyes steadily on the floor. No emotion showed on his face. It seemed sculpted in marble. And something seemed to shrivel and die inside her. He wouldn't look at her. He thought she had done it. Penny jerked her eyes from him. She stared blindly ahead. He couldn't bring himself to meet her eyes. He believed what Matron was saying. He couldn't help her; wouldn't help her. She was utterly alone. Matron made a little movement.

Penny looked at her. 'I have no explanation,' she said, in almost a whisper. 'But I do deny it. And I will forever.'

Penny hardly heard when Matron told her she could go, and that she would let Penny know what was to be done after lunch. She only knew she was dismissed, and she stumbled from the room, the tears already blinding her. But she didn't give way completely to her feelings until she'd gained a secluded corner of the hospital grounds. There she abandoned herself to something like despair.

How could he? How could he believe it? was the cry that echoed in her brain. Beyond the horror of the accusation, of dismissal, of even the loss of her career, was that greater and inextinguishable agony—the agony of knowing that he believed in her guilt, and would not even look her in the face.

Penny could only find one thing to be glad of over the next terrible days, and this was that Jessie hadn't been there to be hurt by her disgrace. After lunch, the Matron had told her briefly that she was 'suspended pending inquiry', and her misery had been too great to appreciate the kindness and forbearance with which the matron had treated her.

She hadn't been able to face her colleagues. She'd said goodbye to no one but the children, whom she told that she was going on holiday and that she wasn't sure when she would be back. Her self-control had only come close to giving way when Sarah had thrown her arms about her and hugged her.

It was hard to see how she would have survived the next few days had it not been for Carrie. She could not go home to her family. Not yet. Not till she had pieced herself together a little.

Carrie's sorrow for her, and her loyalty and indignation, were balm to her. She didn't believe it for a second. She refused to see how anyone else could believe it. She was angry. She was furious with Nicholas Adams for not defending her.

But, although at times Penny's own anger flared and she also blamed him, her dominant emotion was grief. She was grieved at the accusation, grieved at forfeiting the good opinion of the matron, whom she had liked, grieved at the loss of her job, and being away from the children. But most of all she grieved over Nicholas Adams.

He had said no word to her, had not looked in her direction. That alone communicated his belief in her guilt. For surely, if he had *not* believed it, he must have said so, must have looked at her, spoken to her, let her know she had his faith and support.

He had abandoned her completely. And the thought of that was like a knife in her.

'All I can say is that he must be a rotten judge of character,' Carrie had declared angrily.

And it had fanned Penny's own anger briefly. He knows me! she cried inwardly. He knows me better than anyone there! How could he think that of me? How could he, caring for me, think I am guilty of that?

But perhaps, she was forced to think now, she'd been wrong about that. She'd felt almost sure that he loved her. But 'almost sure' wasn't certainty. Perhaps it was only a physical feeling. He wanted her. Desired her. He wanted to—Penny couldn't bring herself to finish the thought.

Was he disappointed now? Was he sorry for her? Or did he despise her? Feel that he'd had a lucky escape from an involvement with a drug-taker and a thief?

She would never know. For whatever happened, she would never see him again. Whatever he felt about her—contempt or regret—she could never face him again.

And, despite how he had hurt and angered and shamed her, Penny thought suddenly that this was the bitterest part of all. He was gone from her life. In the midst of her ruined career, in the face of her certain belief that no 'inquiry' could do anything to help her, the death of the hope she had cherished was the worst blow to her. For if he *had* cared at all, it was over now. Now he would never care, not for the sort of person he believed her to be.

Nicholas Adams was straight as a die. He couldn't care for that sort of person. And for that, at least, Penny could not blame him.

The loss of it wrung her. His eyes haunted her, and

his smile. His tenderness and humour with the children, his hands as they worked, the way he had of watching intently while you spoke that had so disconcerted her—all came back to fill her dreams and her days with greater anguish.

Larry had rung on the first night—at least, she supposed it was Larry. She had expected it and, as soon as she'd heard the telephone ring, had known she couldn't bear to speak with him.

'Carrie, tell whoever it is that I've gone home to my parents, please?' she begged. 'I don't want to speak with Larry. I don't want to speak with anyone.'

Carrie had done it, and the man, gently, seeming to understand, had said no more than, 'I see. Thank you'—with a note, Carrie thought, of regret.

Perhaps he hadn't believed her, for the next day, when Carrie was at work, the phone had rung again. Penny had pulled the cord out from the socket to stop it. In a few days, her greatest wish was to be at home with her family.

But there was a problem. She had promised Jess she would see her, and she couldn't see how she could break that promise and run away.

So she spoke to her family instead, and a sorrowful conversation it was for the Anderson family. Her father was deeply grieved, and shocked.

But it gave her some comfort to know that he thought she had done the right thing in not accusing Berensen.

'It would be a terrible accusation to make,' he agreed, 'without any evidence. As terrible as the deed itself.'

And above all comforting was the implicit certainty

of those who loved her that she had not done as she had been accused.

It gave her the strength to compose herself and to ring the number that Mrs Brand had given her. She spoke to Jess on the phone, and promised to come the next day.

'Have you heard anything from the hospital?' Carrie asked her tentatively when she arrived home that evening.

Silently, Penny indicated the plug of the telephone, and Carrie gave a rueful smile.

'I'll plug it in again, shall I?' she said. 'I can answer it. And they might want to contact you. Maybe their inquiry will turn something up. . .'

Penny had no hope of it. 'It's her word against mine, Carrie,' she pointed out. 'There's no way of proving it.'

Carrie poured the tea and sat down. 'You know,' she said, 'I've been thinking about that. Maybe, just maybe, there is *one* way.'

Penny waited.

'Well,' her friend went on, 'we've been assuming that Berensen swiped the drugs to get rid of you. But—but, Penny, what if she was actually *taking* them?'

Penny frowned. 'I hadn't thought of it,' she admitted. 'I suppose it's possible. She might have been taking them herself. And it was also a convenient way to get rid of me.'

Carrie nodded.

'But I don't see how it helps,' Penny said. 'There's no way of proving she was taking them. And it—it hardly matters what she did with them. They still think it was me. And I can't prove it wasn't.'

'But it might matter, Pen,' said Carrie decidedly. 'Remember what was missing. They're addictive drugs. If Berensen has been taking them, she might not be able to stop just like that.'

Penny stared at her for a moment. 'Good Lord! You're right. I—I suppose there *is* just a chance that she's addicted to them. If that were so——'

'She'll need to take more,' finished Carrie.

Slowly, Penny shook her head. 'I don't think I can pin my faith on that, Carrie. She probably wasn't taking them herself. She probably just stole them to implicate me. And even if she is one of those nurses who uses drugs, she may only do it from time to time. And she'd be a fool to take any more. Whatever else she is, Carrie, I don't think she's a fool.'

'Hmm,' Carrie mused. 'Well, you're right. She'd have to be very careful about taking any more. They'll certainly be watching them. But there *are* ways to do it. You can give the patient only half the dose you write down, and pocket the rest.'

Penny frowned. 'She wouldn't do that, Carrie. That's an awful thing to do. That would mean the patient wouldn't get enough of the drug to get rid of the pain.'

'Pen, I think it's time you realised that this lady doesn't have your principles. Anyway, an addict will basically do almost anything.'

'Well, even if she does,' argued Penny, 'they'd have to watch her awfully closely to realise she was doing that.'

'Yes. I agree with that.'

'And why should they? They've already found the culprit.'

Carrie narrowed her eyes. 'Don't be so sure they won't, Pen,' was all she replied.

But the faint hope which this thought raised in Penny didn't live in her long. And it was Larry Stevenson who extinguished it. An hour later, he knoced on their door. There was nothing for it but to admit him. He flung himself down beside her on the sofa and gave her a comprehensive hug.

'Thanks, Larry,' she said at last, extricating herself and introducing him to Carrie.

It was Carrie who asked him what was happening with the inquiry, for Penny found herself unable to speak of it.

Larry was silent a moment. 'Look,' he began at last, 'I don't want to make things worse, but I think you ought to know, Pen, that the inquiry isn't likely to help you much.'

Penny raised her eyes to his face. 'That's what I thought,' she said, 'but then Carrie had the idea that someone might be stealing them because they're addicted.'

Larry smiled grimly. 'I'm sure I know who it was that nicked them, Pen. A lot of us are sure of that. But whether she's silly enough to be addicted, I don't know. And even if she is, I don't think the inquiry is going to be vigorous enough to detect it. You see, you don't seem to have the right people on your side.'

Penny's face became a little pale. 'W-what do you mean?'

'Our unit director doesn't appear to share our faith in you,' he said, and it was almost with satisfaction.

'He's let it be known that he's satisfied the culprit has been found. I don't think the nursing administration will look at it too much harder. He's got a lot of influence, you know.'

And now there was so little colour left in Penny's face that Larry felt alarmed.

'Are you OK?' he asked, and she nodded. 'I didn't mean to upset you, my dear girl. But you must know the truth about Nick and face it. He has a façade of caring, of humanity. But he's really totally cut-off and unfeeling. Anyone with any human understanding would have known you're incapable of doing what they say you've done. But Nick. . .' He shrugged. 'I just didn't want you to have any illusions that he's going to help you, sweetheart.'

'I don't have any illusions, Larry,' she murmured, so softly that they hardly heard.

That night, as she lay in bed, Penny reflected how strange it was that one could feel such shame when there was no guilt. For that *was* what she felt, apart from the hurt of it.

She had known that he was convinced of her guilt. It had been the only explanation for his behaviour. And yet she realised now that she must have been hoping still—hoping that he was not *quite* certain, or that he would change his mind. Now she must face it fully. He *was* convinced. Nicholas Adams, who she respected more than any man, thought her a thief, a drug abuser, a liar. There was no way of ever proving to him that he was wrong.

And the shame of it made her face burn and her heart ache. The only comfort she could conceive of was never to have to see him in her life again. And, given those other feelings she had, those feelings for him which would never go away, it was cold comfort indeed.

CHAPTER ELEVEN

PENNY caught a bus next morning to go and see Jess.
It was a slow way to travel. The bus took half an hour,
and wound its way rather indirectly through the sub-
urbs, but it stopped quite conveniently, leaving Penny
across the road from her goal. She was glad to see, as
she stepped up to the door of the house, that it was set
in a pleasant garden, and that there was an air of
tranquillity about the place.

Even more was she pleased when Mrs Brand greeted
her affectionately and showed her out to a back garden
that was full of spring flowers and sunshine. Jess was
sitting in the sun in a chaise-longue, and she had no
need to tell Penny she was happy to see her.

'Isn't it lovely here, Penny?' she said when they had
hugged sufficiently.

'It's perfect,' agreed Penny, and meant it.

'There's a cat here, Penny. It's Mrs Ingram's.
Mummy's friend. We're looking after it. It's called
Sooty.' And she sat forward and called, 'Puss, puss,
puss. Where are you, Sooty?'

Penny noticed that the exertion tired Jess, but she
leaned back again, happy, when a grey face appeared
among the hydrangeas to see whether this might mean
food.

There were books on the grass beside her, and a
game she had been playing with her mother on a low
table. It was so much better for them than the hospital.

155

If only the hospital had a place like this, Penny thought, for children like Jess and their parents to come to. She had almost begun to wonder how one would begin to get an idea like that off the ground when she recalled that very soon she would no longer be on the payroll of the hospital.

'Are you very busy at the hospital, Penny?' asked Jess. 'You look tired.'

'Oh—no,' said Penny. 'I mean—they are, but I'm having a holiday.'

'Oh, Pen, good! That means—oh, but—I guess you must have a lot to do in your holidays.'

Penny smiled at Jess's quick recovery and the unselfishness it spoke. 'No,' she said. 'All I'm going to do is rest, I think. And if you'd like me to be here sometimes, Jessie, I think this would be a lovely place for it.'

And Penny felt happier than she had for days to realise she could still contribute so much to one person's happiness.

She had only meant to stay a few hours. Penny was acutely aware of how little time the Brands had left with their daughter, and didn't want to intrude on it. But they seemed to be glad to have her there. And, after a lunch on the lawn, she found herself playing diplomacy with Neil and Ellen Brand and Jess with quite a degree of hilarity.

The shadows had begun to lengthen on the grass and Sooty to complain that it was his dinner-hour when she finally took her leave, and that was with a promise to return tomorrow in the afternoon.

'You mustn't let her talk you into giving up all your holiday, Penny,' Ellen said to her at the door. 'It's so very kind of you, but I know you must have things you'd rather do.'

Penny shook her head. 'No, Ellen. There's nothing in the world I'd rather do. I've come to love your daughter, you know. But I don't want to butt in, either——'

Ellen didn't let her finish. 'You'll never be doing that,' she cried. 'If you know how happy it makes us to see her laughing with you. . . And—we're afraid at times, Penny. If—something were to happen. We wouldn't know what to do. It makes us feel more confident. . .'

It was only when Penny was sitting on the bus again that she reflected that in a very short time she would no longer have the opportunity to get to know people like the Brands. In a very short time she would not be a registered nurse at all.

Penny visited again the next day as promised. The following one was Saturday, and she spent it once again with Carrie on the harbour. The day, while promising fair, had turned out stormy, and they had quite an exciting time in the squalls.

It was good for Pen, Carrie thought, to have all her mind on not capsizing in front of a ferry. She seemed more cheerful today, even when a sudden downpour drenched them and they ended up shivering with cold while they unrigged the dinghy at the boat ramp.

It was something to tell Jess about the next day. Penny made it into a funny story, and much maligned her skill as a sailor in the process. Jess was delighted, especially with Penny's description of herself when she got home after slipping in the mud on the ramp.

But Jess also had something to tell, and the hearing of it took all Penny's self-control.

'Dr Nicholas was here, Penny. He came yesterday. He had lunch with us, and it was so nice. And he played a game of cards with us, too. Wasn't that nice of him?'

Penny had to agree. She had wondered when Nichlas Adams would find time to come and see his patient. House calls weren't usual in his branch of the profession. It was certainly generous of him to give up his Saturday.

'He's terribly handsome, isn't he, Pen?' said Jess.

Penny felt a hand squeezing her heart. But she managed to answer, 'Yes. Yes, he is, Jess.'

'You do think so, then?' asked her friend.

Penny contrived a gay smile. 'Oh, no doubt about it, Jessie. You couldn't have had a more handsome date.'

'And he's kind too, don't you think, Pen?'

It occurred to Penny to wonder for a moment whether there was any special reason for this painful cataloguing of Nicholas Adams' virtues, but banished the thought almost immediately. Jess was just admiring him, just enjoying thinking about a friend with whom she had very little time left.

Penny agreed again and, by dint of reproaching herself for her selfish weakness, managed to hold her end of a discussion of the perfections of the man she loved beyond all others but could never have.

'I told Dr Nicholas you were here, Pen,' revealed Jess at length. 'He was surprised. He thought you might have gone home to your family. Pen, you're not just staying here because of me, are you?' She looked troubled.

Firmly, Penny shook her head. 'I'm staying here because I want to, Jess. It's not the best time of year to visit my parents. Most of my brothers and sisters are at school in term-time.'

Jess was relieved, and they spoke once more of Penny's family, and what it was like to have so many brothers and sisters. Penny told her all the funny and interesting stories she could think of about them, and the time passed so quickly that Penny almost missed her bus.

So Nicholas Adams had expected her to leave the city. Well, she probably ought to have done. What was the point in hanging around here, after all, hoping for a miracle? He was convinced she was responsible for the theft of the drugs. Nursing Administration would be satisfied. No evidence to the contrary existed. There was no hope. There would be no reprieve, no rein-statement. But she was surprised he could think that she would break her promise to Jess.

And then it came to her again what sort of person he thought she was, and she was surprised no longer. She only felt the agony of that burning shame again, and the ache of her loss. And now she promised herself that as soon as she could she would leave this city and find a place where she might never risk coming face to face with Nicholas Adams again.

'Pen,' Carrie called her over the banisters. 'Larry called. He's going to call again.'

Penny groaned. She couldn't bear it. She just wanted to be alone, or to sit with Carrie and be quietly miserable.

'He might cheer you up,' suggested Carrie, but Penny gave her a look that put this hope to rest. 'No. OK. Well, I'll tell him—ah——'

'Tell him I've got a migraine,' said Penny. 'It's not too far from the truth.'

It wasn't long before the telephone rang, and Carrie ran to pick it up, her story prepared.

But it wasn't Larry Stevenson on the line. The caller gave his name as Nicholas Adams before he asked for Penny.

Carrie was immobilised for a moment. She was in the hall. Penny was in the sitting-room. Would Penny want to speak to him? But she recovered herself quickly.

'Ah, look, I've just walked in the door,' she said. 'I'm not sure whether she's here or not. I'll just go and call her.' She dropped the phone, and shut the sitting-room door behind her.

'Pen, it's not Larry. It's Nicholas,' she said, and watched her friend's face turn from white to scarlet.

'Tell him I'm dead,' she said, and Carrie couldn't repress a chuckle.

But she quickly became serious. 'Pen, he might have some news. It might be worth talking to him'

'No!' cried Penny. 'If there were any news I wanted to hear, Matron would call me. I c-can't—Carrie—I can't bear to talk to him. Ever.'

Carrie could see that she meant it. And she couldn't blame her. This was the man who was so sure of Penny's guilt.

'I'll tell him you've got a migraine,' she said softly, and went to suit the action to the words. She wondered for a moment whether he was still there when she told him. There was a silence.

But then he spoke. 'I'm sorry to hear it,' the deep voice said.

Carrie could hear that he didn't believe it, but reflected that it served him right. 'Can I take a message?' she asked, and there was another pause.

Finally, he spoke again, and the gentleness of his voice surprised her. 'No,' he said. 'Thank you. But I hope she'll feel better soon. Take care of her.'

Frowning, Carrie replaced the receiver, and went to speak to her friend. 'Pen,' she said. 'I think you ought to have spoken to him.' Penny shook her head. 'Don't you want to know what he wanted?'

'It doesn't matter what he wanted!' Penny cried. 'He thinks I'm a drug thief—that's all that matters.'

Carrie frowned again. 'Pen, he sounded—sorry. And—well—nice. . .' And at once she regretted saying it, as Penny buried her face in the sofa and cried.

But she couldn't leave it there. 'Perhaps you're wrong, Pen. Perhaps Larry's wrong. Perhaps he doesn't believe it. . .'

Penny's only answer was a sob.

Later, however, she thought about it, though not to any positive conclusion. Why had he rung? she asked herself. What could he have to say to her? Matron had told her she would phone if anything came of the inquiry. From that quarter, she had heard nothing.

Could he be uncertain? No, it wasn't possible. One thing she did know of Nicholas Adams. He would never have confided his belief in her guilt to others if there had been any doubt in his mind at all.

And uncertain wasn't good enough, she reflected. Only a whole-hearted belief in her innocence would satisfy her, the same unshaken and unshakeable conviction that her parents felt.

Then why would he call? The question reiterated itself. Could he still feel that—that want of her, in the face of everything? The thought made her colour.

And she didn't believe it. He wouldn't want anything to do with her now, not even physically.

And suddenly an explanation presented itself. Perhaps he had called about Jess. Perhaps—perhaps he didn't want her to see Jess any more—a person like her, no longer a hospital employee. . . It seemed possible. And it made her feel glad that she hadn't given in and spoken to him. Because nothing was going to stop her from seeing Jess—not even Nicholas Adams at his worst.

The shadows were once more long upon the lawn when next day Penny got up to leave Jess. She had meant to go for some time, for Jess seemed more tired than ever today. But it was obvious that she wanted Penny to stay that she'd not had the heart to do otherwise.

'I think Sooty's getting very aggrieved at the lateness of his dinner, Jess,' she joked, and the child gave a sad little smile.

'Yes, poor puss,' she agreed. 'Only I did want you to stay just a little longer, Pen. . .'

The wistfulness in her tone cut at Penny's heart. 'Did you, sweetheart?' she said. 'But I'll be back, you know. . .'

Slowly, Jess nodded, and had just put up her arms

for a hug, when suddenly she stopped, and turned excitedly in her chair.

'That's him!' she cried. 'I know his footsteps. That's Dr Nicholas!'

Penny's heart seemed to stop. The blood seemed to drain from her. She stood as though turned to stone. Such was Jess's gladness to see her other friend, she didn't notice.

But Nicholas Adams couldn't fail to do so.

In a moment he had covered the space of the lawn with his long stride, and stood before her. His eyes swept her face, even as he reached out to Jess for a hug.

For a space there was no opportunity to speak. Jess was telling him how glad she was to see him, and how they had spent the afternoon, and Mrs Brand had come outside to welcome their visitor and offer a cup of tea. But all too soon he had turned to Penny again, and she knew that she had to escape. The pain was too great to bear. For one split second as he had stood before her, she had allowed her eyes to flick up to his face. It had been enough. She knew in that instant that she loved him as much as ever, and that her decision never to see him again had been wise.

Almost without knowing it, Penny began to speak. Her voice was taut and unnatural. 'I must go,' she said. 'I'll miss my bus. It's——'

'Oh, no, Pen!' cried Jess. 'Not when Dr Nicholas is here. Just stay a little while.'

'You must have time for a cup of tea,' she heard Ellen saying. 'It's all ready.'

And she knew that she had to control herself. She couldn't let them realise how upset she was. Jess would be so concerned. And how could she explain it to them?

Heavily, she sat down in her chair. 'Well, I—I suppose I could stay——'

Penny found she couldn't complete the sentence. But it was good enough. Jess clapped her hands.

'Mummy,' she said. 'Daddy will be home soon. Maybe he could run Penny home?'

'Of course he could——' Ellen Brand began, but Penny hurriedly began to decline the offer.

Jess and Ellen combined against her in good-natured argument until Nicholas Adams cut across it and delivered the *coup de grâce*. '*I'll* take Penny home,' he announced quietly.

Penny struggled for command of herself, for the ability to behave as naturally as possible. With a supreme efort, she forced herself to answer him casually, aided greatly by the reappearance of Sooty, who had come to rub himself against her legs. She bent down to stroke him, and spoke at the same time.

'That's kind of you, Dr Adams, but it's really not necessary. There's a bus in half an hour.'

'Nevertheless,' she heard him say, 'I'll take you home.'

Penny felt her heart lurch. There was no mistaking the decision in his voice. He was determined to speak to her.

Penny's anger rose up in her. Well, he wouldn't. She wouldn't hand him an opportunity to forbid her to keep seeing Jess. If she had to resort to straight-out flight, she would avoid that.

The next half-hour seemed an eternity, as she listened to Nicholas Adams answer Jess's questions about the ward. His deep voice stirred her as ever, and that dry humour which made Jess laugh so delightedly filled her with an unaccountable urge to cry.

'You must miss Penny,' Jess observed to him, and there was a pause during which Penny had physically to force herself to go on calmly stroking the cat which had now taken up residence in her lap.

'We do,' she heard him say at last. 'We all do.'

Penny felt more miserable, if anything, at the polite lie.

Finally, her frequent glances at her watch told her that the bus would be here in five more minutes. She had managed to swallow a cup of tea that had tasted like ashes and water, and had managed to make a little desultory conversation with Ellen, all without once turning her eyes to within three feet of Nicholas Adams. She felt she had done very well. But now was the hardest part.

Penny evicted Sooty from her lap, and stood up. 'Thank you, Ellen. I really must go now. Carrie will be expecting me.' She turned to Jess and hugged her.

'You'll come again soon, won't you, Pen?' Jess asked.

'Of course I will,' she answered. 'No matter what.'

If Nicholas Adams perceived the challenge in that remark, he showed no sign of it. He merely stood up and stepped forward. 'The car's quite close,' he said quietly.

Penny thought rapidly. She was not going to do anything to alarm Jess and Ellen. 'Thanks,' she said brightly, and glanced in his direction, though her glance didn't reach as far as his face.

A moment later they were out on the road. Thankfully, Nicholas Adams hadn't yet spoken. Penny anxiously scanned the road for the bus, and with a sigh of relief saw it was two stops away.

Abruptly she turned to him, her heart hammering and her face flushing scarlet. 'There's no need for you to drive me,' she said. 'My bus is here.'

'I want to drive you,' he replied. 'I want to speak to you.' Penny shook her head and stepped back.

'Penny!' He made a movement towards her. His voice commanded her.

'No!' she cried, stepping back off the kerb.

He stopped a moment. 'Penny, please——' His voice was urgent now, and strained.

'No, no, no!' she cried, half sobbing, and before he could complete his lunge towards her had turned and fled blindly across the road. One car braked and another hooted as Penny hurled herself towards the waiting bus.

She caught one last glimpse of Nicholas Adams as the bus pulled away. He had turned away and was leaning against his car.

'Penny, that was stupid,' Carrie scolded. 'He wants to speak to you. You may be wrong about him. I've been thinking about it all day. I almost think you are.'

Miserably, Penny huddled in her chair. 'I just c-couldn't, Carrie. I had to get away. What if he tries to stop me seeing Jess? I couldn't bear that. Anyway, I just can't speak to him. It's too painful. It's too much to expect.'

Carrie sighed. 'Penny, I'll give you my advice. If he

tries to contact you again, you'd better listen to what he's got to say. It might be important.'

And at six the next morning, Nicholas Adams did contact her again. Carrie was up already, getting ready for work. She shook her friend awake.

'It's Adams on the phone, and this time you've got to speak to him,' she said firmly.

'No!' gasped Penny.

'Yes!' cried Carrie. 'Penny, yes!' She hauled her friend out of bed.

Penny stood beside the phone for a long moment, looking imploringly at Carrie.

Finally, Carrie picked it up and put it in her hand.

Penny swallowed hard. 'Hello,' she said faintly. Her lips were dry and her heart thudding.

But it was not what Carrie had hoped for.

It was Jess. She was back in hospital, and dying.

CHAPTER TWELVE

THERE had been no question in their brief conversation about whether Penny would come in to be with Jess. Nicholas Adams had assumed she would come immediately. Penny was both surprised and grateful. She had no right at all now to be in the ward. But she would have fought the entire hospital staff to be there. Nothing else mattered now.

The glances of the nurses, curious and sympathetic, were lost on Penny as she hurried along the corridor once more, and found the single room where Jess was to die.

Her parents were there. Wordlessly they reached out hands to her, and she took them for a moment. Their faces conveyed all there was to say.

Jess lay back in bed with her eyes closed, the early light from the window falling on the translucent skin of the little face. For a moment Penny thought she was too late, and felt her heart plunge within her. But then the child spoke.

'That's you, Penny,' she said, her voice slow and indistinct. 'I know your footsteps.'

Penny leant down to hold her.

'Don't leave me, Penny. I'm frightened. To be alone.'

'You're not alone, sweetheart,' she answered, willing her voice to be calm and steady. 'We're all here. You'll never, ever be alone.'

As the sun climbed above the windowsill and into a cloudless spring sky, Jessie lay with those who loved her near by. She drifted at times into a light coma, then surfaced again to seek the comfort of a hand, a dear face, or a few words.

The tumour now had invaded new parts of the brain, and was pressing on those parts essential for maintaining life. Her breathing became uneven. She discovered she could no longer see, and the courage with which she bore it was heartbreaking in itself. 'It's OK,' she managed to say. 'I can see you all—in my—heart.'

Penny thought of Jess's short life as she sat, and knew that the grieving mother and father thought of it too. So bright a promise. So short a space. So cruel and early an end.

How cruel for these loving parents to lose this only child of theirs. It had been cruel enough for her own parents when Meg died. And they had had other children. Penny found herself remembering now, with a vividness she would not have believed was possible, that other time. She felt again the intensity of that earlier pain. And she grieved again for Neil and Ellen Brand, realising how much worse their pain must be.

The matter of the drug theft seemed to have dwindled into insignificance. Had she wept about that, only last night? But what was that, when here was a child slipping inexorably towards death, with courage as bright as the afternoon outside?

It didn't trouble her when Nicholas Adams came in, straight from Theatre in his theatre gown. She was glad. He was so gentle, yet so strong. Even death seemed less frightening while he was there.

Jess seemed to feel it, too. With words becoming

more difficult every moment to frame, she asked him to hold her, and he did.

She struggled to speak again. She was saying his name.

'Yes, Jessie, I'm here,' he whispered. 'I'm listening.'

'Take–care of–Penny,' she managed. 'I love her.'

Nicholas Adams' voice was soft but distinct in reply. 'I will,' he said. 'So do I.'

Penny felt her heart lurch and the blood rush to her face at what he had said.

But through her embarrassment and her pain, Penny felt a glow of gratitude that he could put all personal feelings aside like that to comfort a dying child.

He couldn't stay long. Very soon he was gone, and Jess seemed to feel it a signal. She struggled to say her goodbyes. Penny left for a while, and stood in the corridor.

There was a nurse there, who smiled at her sadly.

After a time, Ellen Brand called her back in, her eyes red-rimmed, but still holding back her grief.

'She wants you,' Ellen said.

Jess didn't speak again, but an answering pressure to Penny's hand on hers told her that Jess knew she was there. And, ever so little, Jess smiled.

Finally, as the sun curved again towards the earth, the child left the shadowed room, and the grief of those who mourned her broke at last in the emptiness left behind.

Penny stayed with the Brands. Knowing she must comfort, she smothered her own grief, though a physical pain burned in her chest. They wept, and talked, and were silent in turn. And, at last, when it seemed they had finished for the time being, Penny offered to come and see them in a few days. Her job at the hospital might be finished, but she would see this through to the end.

It was almost dark when they left. Penny went back into the room where Jess lay, and sat there a while, dull-eyed, motionless, the pain burning still in her chest.

Nicholas Adams took her by surprise. A sound made her look up, and she started a little when she saw him standing before her.

She gave him one quick glance, then looked away again to where her eyes had been.

Jess lay there still, her eyes closed, her face for the first time devoid of expression.

Nicholas Adams knelt down before Penny, his eyes on her face. Slowly he took both her hands in his own and just as slowly drew her towards him. Penny responded like a waxen doll, offering neither co-operation nor resistance. Finally he slid his hands up her arms and round behind her, and held her to him with infinite gentleness.

Numbly, Penny let her cheek rest against the man's shoulder, her eyes never wavering from the dead child's face. And at last she began to cry—quietly first, then with great wrenching sobs that tore from her and shook her whole body.

The room was dark now. In obedience to Nicholas Adams' order, no one had come to disturb them. Penny was quiet and still. The man eased his cramped position a little, wondering if she had fallen asleep at last, but she stirred then, raised her head from where it rested against his neck.

She sat back a little, and he allowed his arms to drop.

'It's dark,' she said, and he rose at that, and switched on the dim night-light.

Her eyes flicked one last time to the child on the bed, then away.

Penny's face was blank. 'You're kind,' she commented, but there was no expression in her voice. And then, all at once, she sat forward and stood up. She raised her eyes to him briefly. 'I have to go now,' she said, in almost a whisper.

'Let me——' the man began, but she shook her head, and moved towards the bed. She stood there a moment, then slowly bent and kissed the pale little brow.

'Bye, Jess,' she whispered, and turned to pick her bag up from the floor.

Nicholas Adams came and put a hand on her arm then. 'Penny, I must——'

But she shook her head again. 'Nothing matters now,' she murmured.

He let her go.

And, in the room where the child had lain dying, it was Nicholas Adams' turn to sit silently. He appeared to be wholly absorbed in his thoughts, perhaps to be wrestling with a problem that wouldn't come right. Then his face took on a new look of determination and, with the air of a man who had made a decision, he got up and strode out to the ward. There he sought and found Belinda Beresen and, after a brief exchange, walked with her towards his room.

CHAPTER THIRTEEN

IT WAS in the loving circle of her family that Penny looked for and found comfort in her grief. In sharing it with them, and telling them of Jess and in remembering Meg with them, her sorrow found balm. She was only away three days, but Carrie could see how much calmer and stronger she was on her return. It was a Penny strong enough to visit the Brands and comfort them anew, and to discuss Jess's death with Carrie with the beginnings of acceptance.

'It will grieve them for the rest of their lives,' she said. 'But Jess got her courage from Neil and Ellen. They're facing it squarely. And they'll come to an acceptance of it.'

Penny tossed the piece of bread she'd been toasting to Carrie, and stuck another piece on her toasting fork. Winter had returned in the last few days, and they sat in front of a fire.

'I wouldn't be surprised if they adopted a child in a year or two,' she continued. 'Neil said something about it.'

'I hope they do,' said Carrie. 'They sound like loving parents.'

Penny nodded.

'Here,' said Carrie, giving Penny the toast she had buttered, and was glad to see her friend munching it absently. She hadn't eaten much since Jessie's death, or since her suspension, for that matter.

'Pen—it really raked up old memories for you, didn't it?'

'Mm. But, you know, Carrie, that's OK. It doesn't hurt you to grieve again. To remember. Well—it hurts, but it doesn't hurt, if you know what I mean.'

'Fortunately,' replied Carrie, 'I've known you a long time. I do know.'

And for the first time in many days she saw Penny smile.

The relief she felt at this was effectively extinguished by the ringing of the doorbell. 'Who's that?' she asked rhetorically. 'It's ten o'clock.'

'And I'm not ready to receive visitors,' said Penny, indicating her nightie.

'Probably someone who smelled your toast from the street,' remarked Carrie, getting up. 'Don't worry. I'll repel all invaders.'

But she was not quite prepared for the force of this invasion.

Nicholas Adams stood resolutely on the doorstep with the air of a man who had no intention of being repelled.

'I know,' he said, as Carrie opened her mouth to speak. 'She has to catch a bus, is at her parents', has scarlet fever.' His tone was gentle but firm. 'Nevertheless, I must see her. I'm sorry. I will see her.'

Carrie recognised a determined man when she saw one. She looked at him for a long moment. 'She's had enough unhappiness for a while. I'm not really big enough to wrestle with you, but if you're going to make her unhappy I'm prepared to try.'

Slowly, there dawned on Nicholas Adams' face the smile that had melted the heart of a hundred nurses.

'Good girl,' he said approvingly. 'Just the friend I would have chosen for her.'

Then, in a moment, he had stepped forward, pinned both her arms to her side, spun her round and kicked the door shut behind them with his foot.

'As you say,' he said calmly, 'you're not really big enough to wrestle with me.'

'Pen!' called Carrie feebly, but the warning was useless. In another instant his stride had taken him across the hall into the sitting-room, and Carrie was left alone to contemplate the ineffectiveness of her resistance, as he shut the door behind him.

Penny sat facing the fire, turning her toast on the fork.

'Successfully repulsed?' she asked.

'Well—not quite,' Nicholas replied apologetically.

Penny wrenched around on her seat, the toasting fork dropped from nerveless fingers. She stared speechlessly at the man who stood before her.

'She did try,' he explained. 'She even offered me violence, which aroused my admiration. I'm afraid I overpowered her with the aid of the element of surprise.'

Penny swallowed hard. In the context of Jessica's death, the troubles between them had seemed to dwindle to a matter of no importance.

She had felt no discomfort with him then. Too many other feelings of too violent a nature had driven her earlier ones away. But, now that she was recovering, all that was changed. Now that her sorrow over Jess was muted, the grief and anger and shame she had felt on Nicholas Adams' account had re-emerged, and they swept through her now with greater force for having been put aside for a time.

And, if those felings were not bad enough, she also felt embarrassed.

Her face aflame, she plucked at her nightdress, and stammered 'I'm not—not——'

'Yes, I see you're not dressed for visitors,' he said. 'And were I to do the gallant thing, I'd undoubtedly leave. But we both know I lack gallantry at times.'

As if to underline the statement, he kicked Carrie's vacated pouffe over beside her, and unceremoniously sat on it.

'I want to make it clear that I don't give a damn that you're in your nightgown, and that I'm not leaving till I have what I want.'

Penny presented a startled face to him. What could he want? A confession? It was the only thing she could think of.

His face became serious. 'Are you all right?' he asked, so tenderly that it seemed to arouse all over again all the pain she had ever felt over him.

She turned her face way. 'Of—of course. I don't know what you mean.'

'Your friend told me you'd gone home to your family.'

'Wh-when——?'

'Oh, I've rung a great number of times lately without giving my name. It occurred to me that I might have more success that way.'

Penny could think of nothing to say.

'Did it help?' he asked gently. 'Going home? I mean—with Jess.'

She allowed herself to look at him. 'Yes,' she said.

'It helped—it—always does. I'll never forget her. But I can accept it.' She turned to gaze at the fire. 'It was the best sort of death she could have had, I think. The easiest. It—was quick.'

'Have you seen the Brands?'

'Yes. And they told me you had, too. That was nice.'

'I still care about people, Penny.' His voice was low. 'No matter what others may think.'

'It was good of you to come,' she said formally.

'This was not all I came for, Penny.' He paused, but she didn't look up. 'I've also come on Matron's behalf.'

And now she did look round, and fixed her eyes on him, waiting, not daring to breathe.

'You're cleared, Penny.'

And all at once she felt herself go limp with the relief of it. She closed her eyes and let it flood over her, prayers of thanks forming incoherently in her brain. She hugged her knees and rested her head on her arms for a while, savouring the joy of those words.

'Thank you,' she said at last.

'It was another member of the nursing staff. She confessed. She's left now. Matron will be speaking to you in the morning about coming back.'

Penny was very still. Coming back. The words dropped into her consciousness with the weight of stones into a lake. And suddenly she knew that she couldn't come back. She was cleared. That was wonderful. More than wonderful. It meant she could go on working. Find another job, perhaps like this one. In another town, perhaps. But come back—no. Not while Nicholas Adams was there.

Not while she loved him, and he had proved that he

had no love for her by believing her capable of such an ugly act.

'Maybe you should delay a while. Have a holiday somewhere——'

'I won't come back,' she cut him off.

There was a silence for a moment. Penny stared straight ahead of her.

'Why not?' he asked at length, his voice low.

'I don't want to discuss it with you. I just don't want to come back. Please accept my resignation.'

'Penny,' he said, and her heart lurched as she felt his hand on her arm.

She tried to draw her arm away. 'I don't want to talk about it.'

His grasp tightened. His voice was controlled, but she could hear the suppressed emotion in it. 'I've been trying to talk to you for a week and a half. Let me now, for God's sake.'

She didn't reply. The ticking of the grandfather clock sounded loudly in the silence.

'Look at me,' he ordered abruptly.

She didn't move.

'For God's sake, look at me!' he cried.

And suddenly the anger that had been smouldering in her for so long flared up, and she did.

'What can you possibly want to say to me?' she flung. 'A thief—and—and a drug taker.' She couldn't have said more. A lump had risen in her throat and tears pricked her eyes.

It wasn't just the disgrace of the charge, the anger at his believing it. It was also the effect of his presence—the nearness of those penetrating grey eyes and

that serious, beautiful face she'd been unwise enough
to love.

He was answering her. 'Not you,' he said simply. 'I
always knew that.'

And when his words had sunk in, she looked at him
incredulously. What was he saying? He was lying to
her.

'That's not true,' she replied. 'That's not true. You
thought I'd done it from the start. You—you wouldn't
look at me. And I know you thought it because I've
been told. You let everyone know you thought I'd
done it. The only reason I'm cleared is that the person
concerned owned up. If it had been left to you, I'd
never have been cleared.'

Penny's eyes blazed with anger. She drew a breath
and continued, careless now in her passion of what she
said.

'You think all you have to do is say the right things
in that voice, and look at people in that way, and
they'll accept whatever you say. Well, you can't charm
me. I know you thought I'd done it. And you of all
people ought to have known the truth. I don't blame
Matron—she hardly knows me. But you know me.
And you, I'll never forgive.'

Penny wrenched herself round and stared fiercely at
the fire. His hand had dropped from her arm. Perhaps
he'd go now.

There would be nothing more for them to say to
each other. Ever. She was cleared.

She was glad of that—so glad. But she didn't want
him here. He thought so little of her. He didn't care
for her. And, despite everything she felt and all she

had said, she still cared so much for him that she ached
with it.

She heard him give the smallest sigh. Then, before
she knew what was happening, she found herself
pulled off her seat and into his arms. She gasped and
began to fight, but almost before she'd begun his arms
had pinioned her to his chest, one hand forcing her
head back so that she stared into his eyes. She couldn't
move.

'Now listen to me.' His voice was determined. 'No,
don't struggle. It won't avail you. You'll stay there till
you've listened to every word I have to say. I'm not
usually so ungallant as this, but, if it's the only way,
then it has to be.'

Penny found her heart beating wildly, pinned against
his chest and her face only inches from his own. She
smelled again the masculine scent of him, as she had
on those other occasions when he had held her. It
suddenly seemed to her that she might faint, but she
fought against it.

'What you say has no truth in it at all. I never for
one second entertained the thought that you did as
you were accused. I did see that someone else wanted
us to believe so. I also saw that it was going to be a
damnably tricky thing to prove. I could see only one
way of doing it. We had to hope that the thief had
been using those drugs. That she needed them, and
would take more. We had to watch every move she
made, but in such a way that she would never know
she was under suspicion.'

His grey eyes rested steadily on Penny's, and for a
moment the faintness returned.

'The way to do that was to put it about that we were

sure we already had the thief. That wasn't easy. It provoked something of a revolution among the staff. You may not realise how many friends and admirers you've won at the hospital, Penny. I know, because in the last week I've been besieged and abused by most of them.'

For an instant his eyes crinkled up in a smile.

'Well, I've never been popular, so I suppose I'll survive.' He continued. 'Meanwhile, Matron hired a new nurse. It was her job to watch—this—member of the nursing staff——'

'I know who it is,' Penny blurted. 'Belinda.'

Slowly, Nicholas Adams nodded. 'If you knew, why didn't you tell us?' he asked.

Penny attemped to shake her head, without much success.

Nicholas looked at her a long moment, an unfathomable expression on his face.

'You know, you might never have been cleared,' he said at last. 'It didn't work. The nurse saw nothing to implicate Belinda.'

Penny frowned. 'Then how did—why did she confess?' she asked.

Nicholas Adams' mouth folded into a grim line. It was an expression Penny had seen before. It still made her quail.

'I became a little desperate,' he admitted. 'I took steps of my own to establish the truth. I—saw her. Spoke with her. It wasn't pleasant. Had I been wrong, it would have been disastrous. But I wasn't wrong. And she confessed.'

Penny tried to imagine for a moment what that interview had been like, and suddenly decided that she didn't want to imagine it. Belinda Berensen was considerably tougher than she, but she couldn't imagine even Belinda being able to brazen it out in front of Nicholas Adams at his worst, especially feeling about him as she did.

She felt a little rush of pity for Belinda. She understood why the girl had done it. She loved Nicholas Adams so much—as much as Penny did herself.

Penny breathed a long sigh, and closed her eyes. 'I see,' she murmured at last, in a small voice, and with that felt Nicholas Adams relax his grip.

'Good,' he said. 'In that case, if you want, you may escape me.'

What did he mean by that? she wondered. 'If you want'? Awkwardly, she withdrew herself from his arms, and sat down again on her own seat.

For a long while she was silent, thinking of what he had said. Then she raised her eyes to his once more.

'If it's true,' she said in the smallest voice, 'why didn't you look at me at least? Why didn't you let me know?'

Nicholas met her eyes steadily, but there was a new look of pain in his own.

'I couldn't tell you then, in front of the assistant matron, that I believed in you,' he explained softly. 'All I could do was watch you suffer. And in the end I found I couldn't bear to do that. . .' His voice trailed away.

Penny's lips formed a soundless 'oh' as she realised what he was saying.

'And I did try to tell you afterwards. That night, the next day. Many times. You didn't make it easy for me, Penny. On one occasion you nearly ran under a car!'

Penny gave an inner groan. It was true. And all at once it was borne in on her how unfair *she* had been. He *had* believed in her. And endured considerable unpleasantness—exactly the sort of thing he would hate. Abruptly she thrust out her hand and put it on his arm.

He raised his eyes to her quickly.

'I'm sorry,' she said. 'I—I should have believed in *you*. I'm the one who has committed the injustice.'

Slowly she saw him smile that devastating smile, and it made her feel weak. Shyly, she withdrew her hand, only to have him catch it on its return journey and imprison it in his own.

'No,' he said. 'How could you have thought anything else? I knew that there was a good chance that my— belief in your guilt would be reported to you. You have a very staunch supporter in Larry Stevenson.'

Penny stole an anxious glance at him. 'He didn't mean to make trouble. Only—to warn me not to get my hopes up.' She realised that she didn't sound entirely convinced.

Nicholas looked up at her and smiled. 'Oh, he did me a considerable favour. I wasn't sure at first that people would swallow the story that I believed you'd done it. But Larry found it easy enough to believe, for reasons of his own. And that convinced others.'

Yes, she thought, Larry would find it easy to believe. His prejudice would have blinded him to any other possibility.

'Larry Stevenson is a good doctor,' she heard Nicholas say musingly. 'But he needs to get out of my shadow. One day he'll run his own unit, very ably.'

Penny was surprised, and pleased at his generosity.

Larry had done little to endear himself to Nicholas, she thought. And yet——

'Nicholas,' she said quickly, before she could lose her courage, 'have you ever told Larry that?'

He looked at her for a moment, first with faint surprise, then thoughtfully. 'No,' he said at last. 'I don't suppose I ever have.' And he smiled now, a rather rueful smile. 'I suppose I ought to have, eh?'

'It might just help,' she agreed gently.

She felt him squeeze her hand, and saw that slow smile curve his mouth again. 'Are you sure you won't come back, Penny? I don't seem to be doing too good a job running the unit on my own.'

Penny gave a shy laugh. 'Yes, I'll come back,' she said at last.

With that a constraint seemed to descend on them. They sat together for what seemed a long while, Penny's hand still held in his, gazing at the flickering fire.

Then finally Penny felt him turn to her. She looked up. His eyes were on her face, his own face tense. She felt his grip on her hand intensify.

'Penny,' he almost whispered. 'I made Jess a promise. . .'

Penny felt her heart lunge and the colour rushed into her cheeks. 'Oh, you didn't—that was——'

'Did you think I would lie to a dying child?' he asked, his eyes intently holding hers.

Penny couldn't speak. Her heart seemed to stand still completely.

And Nicholas Adams seemed to throw all caution away. Once again he pulled her into his arms, and caught her to his chest.

'Penny,' he whispered hoarsely and, crushing her even closer, kissed her hair. 'I love you so much I ache with it. Don't say you hate me still. I couldn't bear it.'

Penny's heart surged with joy, and danced an even crazier beat.

'I don't hate you—even a little bit,' she managed to say, and was rewarded by threatened suffocation. 'Nicholas,' she said breathlessly, 'I have to breathe. I'm funny like that.'

He laughed and released her a little, and in a moment she found herself once again looking into the grey eyes she had always found so disconcerting.

'I'm sorry, my love,' he said. He sounded breathless too.

She smiled a tremulous smile. 'I——The truth is— I've loved you so terribly for a very long time.'

An expression that Penny had seen before filled Nicholas Adams' face. This time Penny recognised it. All doubt fled from her mind. He loved her, as much as she loved him.

And, in another moment, his mouth, for the second time, had reached her own and was moving on her lips with a passionate urgency that flooded her with fire and turned her limbs to liquid. Her arms went round his neck, and she felt herself cradled against his strength.

'Do I take it I no longer intimidate you?' he asked at last.

Penny grinned. She didn't answer. Instead, she took his face between her hands, and kissed him back.

Nicholas seemed to find it a satisfactory answer. When, finally, the kiss was over, he only smiled that heart-stopping smile, and murmured, 'I see.'

'I wasn't intimidated all the time,' said Penny. 'But I do have a problem with authority-figures.'

Nicholas pressed her against him again and stroked her hair. 'Especially ones who abuse you as I did,' he acknowledged softly.

'Oh, no,' Penny replied quickly. 'That was my fault. I shouldn't have interfered.'

'It was mine,' Nicholas stated uncompromisingly. 'You did right to defend Nurse Lang. I behaved very badly. And I'm ashamed to say my behaviour didn't have much to do with the issue in question.'

Penny looked enquiringly at him.

'I—had seen that you and Larry Stevenson were becoming involved. I—already cared.'

Penny shook her head. 'I was never "involved" there,' she said.

Nicholas smiled. 'I learned that later,' he revealed softly. 'I'm something of an eavesdropper, you know.'

Penny grinned back, and hugged him. He was so wonderful to hug—so warm and strong. For a long moment she allowed herself to revel in the feel of him.

'I was a bother to you,' she said at last, and heard him give a chuckle.

'Yes, you were,' he admitted. 'Though not in the way you mean. I was against employing you at the start. I wanted more clinical staff. And you looked so very young and inexperienced. But it was soon apparent to me that Oscar was right. You were the most valuable addition to the staff we could have had. You've made an enormous difference to the unit, Penny.'

Penny hugged him gratefully.

He continued, 'But, oh, yes, you were a bother.

Almost from the start, you disturbed me. . . I'd built a very effective emotional armour, I think. But it crumbled away before those blue eyes of yours, my love.'

Penny felt him hold her tighter.

'I'll never let you go,' he murmured. 'Do you understand?'

She nodded. Her heart was singing.

'Jess was right,' she heard him say. 'She knew. . .'

Penny raised her face to him. She looked into the depth of those grey eyes and saw the warmth and fierceness of his love there. And she gave him a kiss that was also a promise.

Finally, when it was over, a thought occurred to Penny.

'Nicholas, what have you done with Carrie?' she demanded.

He grinned. 'Oh, I didn't do her too much violence,' he answered. 'Do you think she'll forgive me?'

Penny looked at his face and the smile that lit his eyes, and answered it with one of her own.

'Oh, I think she will, in time. . .' she grinned.

— MEDICAL ♥ ROMANCE —

The books for your enjoyment this month are:

A SPECIAL CHALLENGE Judith Ansell
HEART IN CRISIS Lynne Collins
DOCTOR TO THE RESCUE Patricia Robertson
BASE PRINCIPLES Sheila Danton

♥   ♥   ♥   ♥   ♥

Treats in store!

Watch next month for the following absorbing stories:

MEDICAL DECISIONS Lisa Cooper
DEADLINE LOVE Judith Worthy
NO TIME FOR ROMANCE Kathleen Farrell
RELATIVE ETHICS Caroline Anderson

Mills & Boon

Discover the thrill of 4 Exciting Medical Romances – FREE

BOOKS FOR YOU

In the exciting world of modern
medicine, the emotions of true love
have an added drama. Now you can
experience four of these
unforgettable romantic tales of passion
and heartbreak FREE – and look forward to
a regular supply of Mills & Boon
Medical Romances delivered direct to your door!

❧ ❧ ❧

Turn the page for details of 2 extra
free gifts, and how to apply.

An Irresistible Offer from Mills & Boon

Here's an offer from Mills & Boon to become a regular reader of Medical Romances. To welcome you, we'd like you to have four books, a cuddly teddy and a special MYSTERY GIFT, all absolutely free and without obligation.

Then, every month you could look forward to receiving 4 more **brand new** Medical Romances for £1.45 each, delivered direct to your door, post and packing free. Plus our newsletter featuring author news, competitions, special offers, and lots more.

This invitation comes with no strings attached. You can cancel or suspend your subscription at any time, and still keep your free books and gifts.

Its so easy. Send no money now. Simply fill in the coupon below and post it at once to -

**Mills & Boon Reader Service, FREEPOST,
PO Box 236, Croydon, Surrey CR9 9EL**

NO STAMP REQUIRED

✂--

YES! Please rush me my 4 Free Medical Romances and 2 Free Gifts! Please also reserve me a Reader Service Subscription. If I decide to subscribe, I can look forward to receiving 4 brand new Medical Romances every month for just £5.80, delivered direct to my door. Post and packing is free, and there's a free Mills & Boon Newsletter. If I choose not to subscribe I shall write to you within 10 days - I can keep the books and gifts whatever I decide. I can cancel or suspend my subscription at any time. I am over 18.

EP03D

Name (Mr/Mrs/Ms) _____

Address _____

_____

_____ Postcode _____

Signature _____

Offer expires **31st December 1991**. The right is reserved to refuse an application and change the terms of this offer. Readers overseas and in Eire please send for details. Southern Africa write to Independent Book Services, Postbag X3010, Randburg 2125. You may be mailed with offers from other reputable companies as a result of this application. If you would prefer not to share in this opportunity, please tick box. ☐